Entertaining an Elephant

A novel about learning and letting go

by

Bill McBride

This is a work of fiction. Any resemblance of any of the characters to persons living or dead is strictly coincidental.

First Pearl Street Press Edition

Library of Congress Catalog Card No: 97-91764
ISBN: 0-9656254-0-0 (previously ISBN: 1-56002-650-2)

Pearl Street Press
63 Pearl Street
San Francisco, CA 94103

Cover by Jeff Wagener and Ira Johnson

Dedication

To those who have chosen
to teach love rather than fear

Acknowledgments

Children of Wax by Alexander McCall Smith
Copyright 1989 by Alexander McCall Smith
Used with permission of Interlink Publishing Group, Inc.

A Course in Miracles, Vol I, page 100
Copyright 1975, 1985 Foundation for Inner Peace,
PO Box 598, Mill Valley, CA 94942
Used with permission.

The Dhammapada, translated by Juan Mascaro
Copyright 1973 by Juan Mascaro, page 77
Reprinted by permission of Penguin Books Ltd., London, England.

Ghandi on Non-Violence edited by Thomas Merton
Copyright 1964, 1965 by New Directions Publishing Corporation
Reprinted by permission of New Directions.

"The Pooh Way," from *The Tao of Pooh* by Benjamin Hoff
Copyright 1982 by Benjamin Hoff; text and illus. from *Winnie-the-Pooh* and *The House at Pooh Corner,* copyright 1926, 1928 E.P. Dutton, copyright 1953, 1956 by A.A. Milne
Used by permission of Dutton Signet, a Division of Penguin Books USA Inc.

The Power in You by Wally "Famous" Amos and Gregory Amos
Copyright 1988
Published by Donald I. Fine, Inc.

The Prophet by Kahlil Gibran
Copyright 1923 by Kahlil Gibran and renewed 1951 by Administrators C.T.A. of Kahlil Gibran Estate and Mary G. Gibran
Reprinted by permission of Alfred A. Knopf, Inc.

Seven Arrows by Hyemeyohsts Storm
Copyright 1972 by Hyemeyohsts Storm
Used with permission of HarperCollins Publishers Inc.

Author's Notes:
References and research regarding the teaching of grammar and writing may be found in the following article:
McBride, William L., "Grammar, The Stagnant Standard,"
The High School Journal, November, 1979.

Author photo by Paul Morrow

"A clever mind is not a heart.
Knowledge doesn't really care. Wisdom does."

from *The Tao of Pooh*
by Benjamin Hoff

Week One, Day One

For the hundredth time that day, Mr. Reaf listened to the groan of the rusty hinges on the metal door as it slammed shut. The walls of the quonset hut shuddered. He watched the door, expectantly, fearfully. Outside, the voices of the students faded away. Nothing entered but silence. Finally, his time had come. The door remained shut, and what was left of him was for him alone.

On the old wooden desk before him lay five stacks of papers, each stack folded lengthwise and bound with a rubber band, ready to spring open when and if he decided to check the contents. Shoving the papers aside, he rolled back in his chair and plopped his feet on the desktop. Taking a long deep breath, he stretched his arms upward. The ache in his neck spread across his shoulders.

A new year, an old ritual. He stared down at his hands, folded in his lap. His fingers were yellow with chalk dust. Right fingers count wins; left fingers are losses. First period: easy. What a blessing, he thought. Starting the day with Honors. Thank God for that. They'll do anything for a grade. Count one on the right hand for a win.

Next, second period. Average kids. A few talkers. No problem, though. Mostly girls, and they looked scared. He could squelch the chatter quickly enough. Count another right finger. Two wins.

Third period. Average-to-below-average kids. They looked dead--no light in their eyes. No questions. Probably not much upstairs. They're that third quartile in the great bell curve of life, running assembly lines, waiting tables. Reaf knew he wouldn't have many problems with these kids. That's another win.

Next was lunch and Study Hall. He didn't count those. Then fifth. Damn.

Fifth period could be real trouble. He had a rough time quieting them down for roll call. Bad sign. And they whispered throughout their seatwork. Another red flag. He wondered how many could read. Forget writing. Forget homework. Forget class discussion. But there were some athletes. That could mean some leverage with a coach. He stared across the room at the blank chalkboard. They weren't a clear win for him. He'd give it to them today. A left finger uncurled.

Then sixth. Trouble with a capital *T*. His stomach was still in a knot. What a way to end the day, he thought. A room full of them. No manners. No respect. Half look like they're on drugs, and they all look like they're in gangs. When that big Hernandez kid told him to chill out, he should have thrown his butt out of class right then. No, better he didn't. It looks bad to send a kid to the office on the first day.

The Johnson girl looked like trouble, too. She and that whole group of girls in the corner completely ignored him when he told them to be quiet. She's one of those angry ones. He could see the hate in her eyes when he yelled at her. He better park his car in the fenced-in area. Why last period? Why did he have to take this group home everyday?

Reaf stared down at his fingers for the final tally--three wins and two losses. Not too bad, he realized. He certainly had started off years with much worse. For tomorrow, he'd crack down on fifth and go for four wins. Forget sixth period. Most of them would probably drop out this year. Those that didn't quit he'd kick out until he got the class down to a manageable size.

The squeak of rusty hinges caused him to look up. The door opened just a crack as someone leaned against it. A small man squeezed through carrying a broom. His white shirt and tan vest accented an olive complexion. His pants were faded black corduroy. With bowed head, he peered up at the teacher from across the room. He looked Mexican or Cuban, some kind of Hispanic, thought Reaf. Whatever, just another Third Worlder stuck in a menial job. Well, someone has to do it. At least this one is willing to work, unlike the good-for-nothings in sixth period who've never worked a day in their lives.

"Excuse me, sir," the little man said in a soft voice. "I don't mean to disturb you. I would like to begin my cleaning with your room, if you don't mind." Smiling, he stepped toward the teacher. Instinctively, Reaf pulled his feet off the desk. As the janitor came closer, Reaf found himself staring into his eyes. They were large and deep brown--a golden brown like polished mahogany. In each shone a small point of light.

Suddenly Reaf realized what the little man had said. Begin in *his* room. Damn, there went his quiet time, his private time at the end of the day. The janitor had him, though. One golden rule of teaching is to stay on the good side of the janitor. Just try to get Pedro here to clean up some kid's puke if he said no.

Reaf looked down at his papers. "Sure, sure, that'll be fine."

"Thank you, sir. I realize you might need a little time to yourself, so I'll be as quick as possible." He nodded and shuffled over to a far corner. A rhythmic swish of straw on wood began.

Reaf wasn't allowed to leave for a half hour, and he decided not to let the janitor run him out. Grabbing the top stack of papers, he removed the rubber band. The papers sprang open in his hands. "Who Am I?--Personality Checklist." His standard opener for fifteen years. At a glance he could tell how much a kid cared about school, how well he or she could read or write, even what the parents were probably like. It wasn't the content of the questions so much. He didn't really care who their favorite music group was. It was how they answered them. Whether they put any effort in the activity or not. Whether they wanted to play the school game or were going to be trouble.

The steady scraping stopped suddenly. He looked up to see the janitor bent over, looking at a set of literature books on a shelf. He turned toward the teacher.

"Excuse me, sir, but do you teach literature?" He paused when Reaf didn't answer. "I have always been a great lover of literature, you see."

Reaf stared at the man, then raised his hands to his face

and began rubbing his eyes. Oh God, he thought, now he's going to ask me about some author he thinks I should know.

The teacher sighed and looked at the janitor. "Well, I'm an English teacher, but mostly I teach writing. I don't do a lot with those books."

The janitor straightened up. "If you don't mind me asking, what books do you use then, sir?"

"I mostly use these grammar books here," Reaf answered, pointing to the bookshelf beside his desk.

He had barely finished speaking before the little man was beside his desk. Looking at Reaf expectantly, he asked, "These, sir?" He pointed to the grammar books on the shelves.

"Yes," the teacher said, leaning back in his chair. "You see, I've been in this business for a long time, and even though these kids have had a lot of schooling, they still don't have the basics. I don't know what those teachers are doing at the lower levels, but these kids can't tell a participle from a noun. So I take it upon myself to make sure they understand grammar. None of the other English teachers spend that much time with it, so it's up to me to hammer it in."

The janitor had taken a grammar book off the shelf while Reaf talked. His eyes skimmed through the table of contents. Then he began to flip rapidly through the pages.

"Excuse me, sir, where is the writing?"

"What?"

"Well, you said you teach writing. I see mostly sets of numbered sentences."

"Yes, that's right." Reaf reached over and took the book from his hands. How dare this foreigner ask him about his work. Reaf didn't ask him where he kept his dust pan. He pointed at the janitor with his left index finger.

"Look, you probably don't understand any of this, but a disciplined course in grammar is a prerequisite to coherent writing."

"So grammar is useful to these students?" the janitor asked politely.

"Absolutely," Reaf said, leaning back in his chair. "As I tell my students each year, knowledge of grammar is key to having a successful life."

The janitor's eyes widened into mahogany marbles. Reaf gathered up the papers on his desk.

"In what ways do your students use this grammar, sir?"

The teacher could see he had started something he didn't want to get into. Pedro here would ask questions till Christmas vacation. He drummed his left hand on the desk.

"Unfortunately, most of them *don't* use the grammar. That's why they're going to be failures, which proves my point. But that's between you and I."

"Me," the janitor said.

"Yes, you."

Who else would I be talking to, thought Reaf. He began stuffing papers into his briefcase, then suddenly realized the janitor had corrected him. It *is* "between you and me." *Me* is an object of the preposition. Embarrassed and angry, the teacher threw the grammar book he had been holding into the briefcase. The janitor seemed to sense his irritation and stepped back.

"Thank you for your answers, sir. I am sorry if I ask too many questions. But you have helped me understand a little about your profession."

"No problem," Reaf replied as he slipped from behind the desk and past the little man. He turned as he pulled on the heavy metal door.

"Have a nice day," Reaf said sarcastically.

Leaning on his broom, the janitor's whole face lit up with a smile. "Why not?" he replied.

"Why not, indeed," Reaf mumbled and let the door slam shut.

Week One, Day Two

"Power rests on the kind of knowledge one holds. What is the sense of knowing things that are useless?"

--*The Teachings of Don Juan*
A Yaqui Way of Knowledge
Carlos Castaneda

Mr. Reaf hated being late to a class. When you're late your students get the jump on you. You walk into a room full of chatter. Meaningless chatter about who's wearing what, who's dating whom, who's crying in the bathroom, who's pregnant now. You never really regain complete control once they've started talking about their own little lives.

The head of the English department, Mrs. Hurren, had cornered Reaf in the hallway just as the bell sounded. As he crossed the campus to his quonset hut, he replayed their conversation in his mind.

"Excuse me, Mr. Reaf. I hate to keep bothering you, but you've got to order those books. Please. The money that was donated by the Boosters Club reverts to the city fund if you don't spend it in the next few weeks."

"I know, I know," he said, trying to inch away from her. "Give me a few days with the new kids to ascertain their ability levels. Then I'll order the books."

"If I might make a suggestion, Mr. Reaf, there's a new thematic series just out. It uses literature as models for student writing. The brochure says the themes are very relevant to the students' lives. I haven't actually seen the books, but . . ."

She went on and on, as heads of department will do. That's how they get their jobs. They are always trying to change something, and principals like that. It makes them look good at conferences.

"Okay, Mrs. Hurren. I'll give you an order in a few days." He turned to leave.

"And Mr. Reaf, one more thing I forgot to tell you. The Debate Club will be meeting in your room after school on a regular basis. They need a quiet area, and your quonset hut is the only space available."

Reaf turned back to face her. What was he supposed to say to the head of the English department? "No, I don't want those intellectual smart alecks cutting into my private time." Do that and see if she ordered him the electric pencil sharpener he had requested.

"That'll be fine, Mrs. Hurren."

* * *

Reaf slapped his roll book on the desk to get first period's attention. No response. He cleared his throat and focused a cold stare at those who seemed the most animated. Joanna Taylor, who sat just inside the door, was talking a mile a minute.

"How can you tell what is useless and what isn't?" Joanna asked the boy across the row. "We're not old enough to judge these things. My daddy says that he didn't see a use for geometry until the architect showed him the plans for the new guest house."

"And did side-angle-side help him read the blueprints?" asked Paul, turning around in his seat to face her.

Reaf laughed to himself. He certainly couldn't ever remember using side-angle-side.

"I guess so," Joanna replied, a bit flustered. "Sure, it must have helped. Why else would he have studied it?"

"And what kind of power did he get from side-angle-side? Did he become Hypotenus Man?" joked Paul.

The class was listening to their conversation by now, and most laughed at that last crack.

"Why couldn't the architect simply explain side-angle-side if it was so essential to understanding the blueprints?" asked a girl behind Joanna. "I agree with Paul. Geometry is stupid."

"Class!" Reaf said loudly.

All heads turned his way.

"May we begin, please?"

"But Mr. Reaf, we did begin," called out Joanna.

"Excuse me, Joanna, but this is English class, not math."

"Don't you want us to discuss the quotation?" she said, nodding toward the board.

In the upper right-hand corner by the door, written in meticulous script, was a quote by Carlos Castaneda. It seemed the Debate Club had left its mark. Reaf read it slowly.

"Well, uh . . . yes. Of course. But now let's go on with our regular routine. Open your grammar books to the review of the parts of speech."

A chorus of moans filled the room.

"Come on now. We need to learn to write. College Boards are coming."

* * *

The rest of the period, and the entire day, went swiftly. At 3:30 Mr. Reaf kicked back with his feet on the desk, hands in his lap. First period. Except for a slow start with that quote business, they were his. One right finger extended.

Most of the other classes didn't even notice the quote. Second and third were dead as usual. He couldn't get anyone to answer questions even when he called on them by name. Oh well, at least they didn't cause any trouble, he thought. Extend two more right fingers.

Then Reaf smiled. But the best victory was fifth! Coming down hard on Ellis at the beginning of the period made his point. They were his from then on. Not bad, four wins and one loss. He began to replay sixth period in his mind and felt his stomach tighten.

"Hey, Mr. Reaf. Why you got a Mexican's name on the board? You kicking him out of school?"

It was Hernandez. So, he would challenge the teacher on

his second day.

"Mr. Hernandez, Carlos Castaneda happens to be a Hispanic author."

"So why you got his name on the board?"

"Because, Mr. Hernandez, he stated the quotation that's written above it."

All heads had been turning from Hernandez to Mr. Reaf. Now they turned to the board. Reaf watched the lips of a number labor through the words, trying to make sense of the quote.

"Would you like to read it aloud to the class, Mr. Hernandez?"

Hernandez slid down in his seat. Ah, just as he thought. He's afraid to read aloud. Now he had a weapon.

"Forget you, man," Hernandez replied bitterly.

"Okay then. Let's get back to nouns."

Reaf might as well have said, "Let's get back to crochet." Mr. Hernandez's bitterness quickly infiltrated the entire room. Little conversations started here and there. In the back corner someone slammed a book on the floor.

"Okay, settle down." Reaf stared sternly at the class.

"Your power is useless, Mr. Reaf," a voice called out.

"Who said that?" the teacher yelled. He rose to his feet. No one answered. An undercurrent of laughter rose from the back of the room. Reaf felt he was losing them. Quickly he assigned two exercises in the grammar book to keep them busy. An uneasy truce began. If he didn't push them, they'd at least stay in their seats. He'd have to put up with the chatter. Retreating to his desk, he pretended to grade papers while they pretended to do grammar, their eyes glancing every few minutes at the clock.

The creak of the metal door brought Mr. Reaf back to the present. Looking across the room he saw the door open slightly. A broom handle protruded through the narrow opening. It had to be that infernal janitor.

"Good afternoon, sir," the little man said as he entered the room. "I trust you had a pleasant day?"

"Yeah, yeah, it was fine."

Reaf lowered his head into his cupped hands and began rubbing his eyes. Would he have to play one hundred questions with this migrant worker every day?

"And how did the grammar lessons go today, sir?"

"They went. Most of them anyway. There are always those who don't want to learn."

"Yes, I see," the janitor said as he shuffled to the back of the room. "Learning often requires letting go."

Now what the hell does that mean? Reaf thought to himself. He watched the janitor begin sweeping between the rows of desks. The little man moved methodically up the aisles, stroking the floor lightly with the broom, back and forth, back and forth. His arms moved rhythmically, like a pendulum. The constant scraping of straw on wood had a hypnotic effect on Mr. Reaf.

The teacher leaned back in his seat, looked around the room, and smiled. He had grown to love this old quonset hut. Yet he could still remember how angry he had been the day the principal moved him out here. He had cursed him that day as he crossed the school commons, heading for the building in the rear of the school where only special-education teachers had taught before.

But over the years this old metal structure had become his refuge. He loved its odd semicircular shape, which made it look like a huge half-buried drainage pipe, its ribbed roof, which rattled loudly in the rain, and its small windows, which let in only a modicum of light. Here he could do anything he wanted to, without other teachers sticking their noses in to see what he was doing, or trying to tell him how to teach. Few came out here now unless they were assigned to.

"Are those the student papers for today, sir?" The janitor had made his way up the row and was pointing at the stacks of papers on his desk. Mr. Reaf jumped at the sound of his voice.

"Yes, practice sentences on the parts of speech," he answered, reaching for a stack of papers.

"How did they do, if I may ask?"

"Well, I haven't graded them *yet!*" he answered sarcastically. "I imagine first period did fine. So did second.

Most of third probably struggled a little, and fifth and sixth did as little as possible."

The janitor leaned against his broom and cocked his head to the side, thinking. "Why do you think these last classes did so poorly?" the little man asked.

"Between you and . . . uh, me, they don't give a damn."

"That is sad, sir," the janitor replied, shaking his head.

Reaf leaned forward and tossed the papers on his desk. "Yeah, it's a pity. I know my stuff, too. I've been teaching grammar for fifteen years. I could really help these kids if they would take advantage of my knowledge."

"Why don't they care, sir?"

Reaf looked up at the janitor, then across the room. The afternoon sun shone dimly through the dirty windows of the quonset hut. "I don't know. I guess most of them probably think school is useless. Something they learned at home. When the parents don't get through school, they usually don't push their kids. A lot of them are illegals anyway and barely speak English. You know, these foreigners come here without any education, looking to get rich quick, and then they find out they've got to do a little work."

Suddenly Reaf realized he might be describing the janitor and glanced down at his desk.

"Oh, I guess some of them work hard," he said quickly. "But it's not my fault they won't learn. I'm a good teacher. I know what I'm doing."

The janitor took a step closer to Reaf's desk. "They must be very frustrated, sir."

"Frustrated!" The word brought Reaf's head up with a snap. "Hell, they don't know frustration. In the next edition of *Webster's* they'll have my picture by that word. Do you know what it's like to teach kids who don't care?"

"Do you always find it so frustrating, sir?" asked the janitor, leaning against his broom.

"Yeah, well, most of the time. It comes with the territory. But that's no reason for me to give in and change. I've been teaching for fifteen years now, and I've got it down. I've worked very hard to develop my teaching system."

"System, sir?"

"That's right, my system."

Opening his briefcase, Reaf pulled out his old, tattered lesson-plan book and tossed it on the desk. It landed with a loud snap. Yellow chalk dust sprayed into the air.

"It's all in here," he said smugly. The little man looked at Reaf, confused.

"Just name a date," Reaf said, leaning back in his chair and folding his hands behind his head.

"A date, sir?"

"Sure, any date during the school year. Just name one."

"September second."

"No, no. Not today. That's too easy. A date in the future. Take February seventh, for example. Now, watch this."

Mr. Reaf leaned forward and picked up the lesson-plan book. Thumbing through the light-green pages, he came to the page marked "February 7" at the top. He then turned the book around and tossed it back on the desk.

"There now. What do you see?" he said, leaning forward.

The janitor leaned over the desk and studied the book for a moment.

"It says 'diagramming indirect objects.' " He looked up at Reaf, obviously still confused.

"That's right. Indirect objects. Come hell or high water, on February seventh I'll be teaching how to diagram indirect objects. I told you I worked hard. It took me years and years to work out this system. But every year now, with only a few minor adjustments because of holidays and assemblies, I know exactly what I'll be teaching on each and every day. Pretty impressive, huh?" Reaf leaned back in his chair.

"It does make an impression, sir," the janitor replied. "How long have you used this system?"

"Gosh, let me think. You know, I guess I started it about seven years ago, when things really started getting bad."

"Bad, sir? How so?"

"Well, teaching, and schools for that matter, used to be a lot different. For one thing, most kids came to school wanting to learn. They did the homework you assigned, they came to class with pen and paper, they showed you respect. Hell, even those who didn't give a damn acted decently on the whole. Sure, you had an occasional troublemaker, but all you had to do was call a parent and things usually got straightened out."

Reaf leaned back in his chair and stared out the small window across the room. "Teaching was fun then. I used to try all kinds of new things with the kids. But as the kids got rougher, more disrespectful, more screwed up, I found I needed to clamp down on them more and more. Finally, about seven years ago we had a young boy shot to death in our parking lot--over a jacket. Can you believe it? I realized something that day. I wasn't teaching any longer in a school. Instead I was working in a war zone. Where I once saw open doorways, I now see iron gates and metal detectors. Where I once saw student hall monitors, I now see armed policemen. Shoot, kids used to get excited about wearing school colors on game day. Now, because of gangs, they're afraid of wearing some colors any day.

"That year I realized I had to start looking after my own survival if I were going to stay in teaching. I had only ten years until retirement. I felt it was worth hanging on. I figured I could take the abuse as long as I didn't take a bullet."

Mr. Reaf looked back at the janitor. He was staring intently at the teacher. "So I developed a new persona. I deadened myself to this job so it wouldn't kill me. I created a teaching system so I could expend my energy on keeping control and surviving from day to day. And, God help me, in six years I'll be out of here."

The janitor stood holding his broom upright, silent. Reaf opened his desk drawer and threw in some red marking pens.

"Don't think I take it easy, though. I work harder than ever. It's just that after a few years I've refined my system. And, generally, it works well. I don't want to give you the idea that I walk on water or anything. But I think I survive better than some of these so-called master teachers around here. It just takes quite a bit of effort to stay on top of these kids."

The little man suddenly smiled broadly, his eyes like large brown walnuts. Reaf looked at him, surprised.

"You think this is funny or something?" he asked defensively.

"Oh no, sir," the janitor said quickly. "It's just your statement reminds me of an old story."

"So, what is it?" the teacher said, grabbing the lesson-plan book and stuffing it back into his briefcase.

The janitor straightened up. "Well, it seems that one day a yogi came across the Buddha sitting by a still pond. The yogi began to tell the Buddha that his own spiritual powers were very great. In fact, he said that his wisdom and power were even greater than the Master's. To prove this, he said that he would walk on top of the water in the pond. The Buddha asked the yogi how he had acquired this skill. The yogi told the Buddha that in order to gain such control, he had practiced eight hours each and every day for fifteen years. To which the Buddha replied, 'Why have you bothered, when for a mere five rupees you could have taken the ferry?' "

The janitor tilted his head back and laughed loudly. Reaf stared blankly at him. The janitor looked back at Reaf and stopped laughing. Suddenly the door opened. A pimply faced kid with glasses and braces stuck his head into the room.

"Excuse me, Mr. Reaf, but Mrs. Hurren said we're supposed to meet in here."

"Yeah, yeah, I know. The Debate Club. Come in. You kids go ahead and argue with each other. I'm outta here."

He threw the day's papers into his briefcase and headed for the door. The debaters scattered like frightened pigeons.

"Good day, sir!" the janitor called out.

Mr. Reaf let the door slam behind him.

Week One, Day Three

In the beginner's mind there are many possibilities; in the expert's mind there are few.

--Zen Mind, Beginner's Mind
Shunryu Suzuki

"Okay first period, quiet down. Let's get out those grammar books."

"But Mr. Reaf," called out Paul, "aren't we going to talk about the quote?"

Reaf stopped thumbing through the first chapter, entitled "Using Nouns," to look up at Paul.

"The quote?"

"Yes, sir, today's quote." Paul nodded toward the board.

He hadn't noticed, but the Debate Club had left its mark again, written in that same meticulous script in the upper right corner of the blackboard.

As Reaf read it to himself, Rachel in the back called out. "I don't agree with that, Mr. Reaf. The more you know, the more questions you always have. Take scientists, for instance. The deeper they explore, the more questions they have."

"That's not the point, Rachel," Paul called out in a none-too-friendly tone. "If you're totally focused in some wacko experiment, you might as well have your head buried in the sand. You won't see anything else around you."

"Well, Mr. Philosopher," Joanna countered. "How does anybody ever accomplish anything if they don't stick with it and become an authority? Are we supposed to be beginners at everything our whole lives?"

Paul swung around in his desk to face his new adversary.

"The quote says 'in the beginner's mind,' Joanna. That just

means to keep your mind open in the same way a beginner does, even if you're absorbed in some save-the-world project."

"Okay, okay," Reaf interrupted. "And I think it's time we began to open our minds to our grammar books."

Everyone groaned. Reaf grinned as he passed out the day's worksheets.

First period went smoothly as always. Everyone dutifully completed the assignment. The rest of the day, however, was what Reaf called "scheduled bedlam." Whenever there was any kind of assembly, one could forget teaching. Today the administration had scheduled some kind of traveling dramatic troupe at second period. Just what these kids needed, thought Reaf, an excuse to get together in large numbers to learn new ways to act out.

Having played the part of "auditorium gestapo" once too often, he had learned to cast himself in the role of hall monitor at the opposite end of the school from the auditorium. There you only dealt with the occasional smoker sneaking about rather than mob control.

Of course the production ran over, so the administration canceled third period and shortened fourth. Fourth period was noisy throughout Study Hall. It never failed, thought Reaf, the more disrupted the class schedule became, the more disruptive the students were. He knew he was in trouble when the Ellis girl burst through the door at the start of fifth, screaming.

"That was the stupidest, tiredest play I ever saw. Like somebody gonna choose to go back to the project when they could be cruisin' in a Mercedes."

Following Ellis through the door were the other four members of her "gang of five," her fellow jocks on the volleyball team who echoed everything she said. They were laughing loudly and performing all kinds of intricate hand-slapping rituals that only they knew. The Carlson girl turned to Reaf and yelled, "Like that chump is gonna turn down a car and getting high. He better get his scared ass back to his mama."

Every head in the room turned his way. A gauntlet had

been thrown. The first curse word spoken aloud in fifth period. How would he react?

"Okay, settle down. Let's get out our grammar books."

Neither Carlson nor Ellis moved toward her seat. He knew immediately he hadn't come off strong enough.

Ellis swaggered up to Reaf's desk. He rolled back a few inches in his chair. "Hey, Mr. Reaf, tell the truth now, if someone offered you a Mercedes just to hold a little stuff once in a while, wouldn't you get out of this tired-ass school?"

Laughter exploded in the room.

"Ms. Ellis," Reaf said, rising to his feet, "we do not use such language in this room. Now take your seat!"

Ellis turned toward the class.

"Mr. Reaf do what his mama do. He be cool and stay in school."

The class laughed loudly. Hands slapped together in the air to encourage Ellis in her attack.

"That's right, Ms. Ellis. I stayed in school."

"Yeah, all your damn life," yelled Carlson.

"That will be enough, young ladies!" he yelled over the laughter filling the room. "Now either take your seats or leave."

"Bye, chump," said Carlson and swaggered out the door. Ellis and the other three girls followed closely behind, giving high fives as if they were walking off the volleyball court at the state championship.

"Good, get out. Get out!" Mr. Reaf yelled as the heavy metal door clanged shut.

"Ms. Carter. Take this note to the office immediately."

"Why me, Mr. Reaf?"

"Don't question me! Don't anyone else in here question me!" he yelled.

Carter came up to his desk. The class watched Reaf's shaking hand scribble a note to the principal. Score one big loss.

By two-thirty, the news was all over school. Five girls told Reaf off and walked out of his class. Needless to say, sixth period was berserk. In the first few minutes of class, Reaf sent two more to the office, then sat at his desk, staring down at a set of papers while the students snickering comments tormented him like flies on a hot day. He listened as one listens to arguing neighbors, catching only bits and pieces of abuse. Finally the bell ended his misery.

Mr. Reaf stared down at the two extended fingers on his left hand. Why, he thought, do the losses carry so much more weight than the wins? It was a rhetorical question. He knew why. Control is the lifeblood of the teacher. And today he donated at least a pint to some bloodthirsty creeps.

"Good afternoon, sir. I trust you have experienced a fulfilling day?"

He hadn't even heard the janitor enter. God, he hated people who sneaked around. First, they sneak into your country. Then they sneak into your jobs, your neighborhood . . .

"Is everything okay, sir?" the man asked, stopping just inside the door. "Would you prefer I start in another room today?"

Reaf realized he was staring at him as one stares at another driver who's just stolen his parking place.

"No, no. Everything's fine," he said, looking down at his desk. "Go ahead, clean. Clean this mess up."

"I will be happy to, sir," the janitor said, moving to the back of the room.

"One day I'm gonna bring a shotgun in here, and then you'll really have a mess to clean," Reaf mumbled.

"Ahhh," said the janitor without turning around. One of those long, all-knowing *ahhh's* that make you want to punch somebody's lights out. He began sweeping.

"Your students did not behave well today?"

"No shit, Sherlock."

The janitor stopped sweeping and turned toward Reaf, his eyes wide.

"What prompted their behavior, if I may ask?"

"Oh, fifth period walked in here all wound up and started mouthing off about this play they saw. Damn, why do they bring that junk in here? That's so damn typical. The administration brings all this do-gooder stuff in here, hoping to change these kids. But it just makes them crazy, and we have to deal with the consequences."

Reaf slammed the grammar book on the desk. Chalk dust mushroomed in the air.

"What was this play about, sir?"

"I don't know. I didn't see it. Something about drugs, I guess."

"It must have touched your students deeply if they became so excited."

"I doubt they even listened."

"Yet they talked about it?" the little man asked as he stepped toward Reaf's desk.

"Hell yeah, they wouldn't shut up about it."

"So then, sir, what was the problem?"

"The problem is that we're in here to learn, not talk about that crap. But the kids don't want to learn. They just want to raise hell."

The janitor leaned on his broom. He was looking at Reaf intently. The teacher glanced down at the papers on his desk.

"Perhaps, sir, that is precisely what they want to talk about."

"What?" Reaf asked brusquely.

"Hell," the janitor said softly.

Reaf looked up at him. Again he found himself staring into his deep brown eyes. You could get lost in them. Rousing himself, he stuffed his papers in his briefcase.

"Well, we're not here to talk about what *they* want to talk about. We're here to learn grammar. Good traditional grammar. It disciplines the mind. Helps kids read better. Improves their understanding of math and their ability to speak foreign languages. Makes writers of them."

"How do you know these things, sir?"

"Because I've taught it for fifteen years. And I see the results. And there's a lot of research to back it, too."

He threw this last part in for good measure. A long time ago Mr. Reaf learned that when trying to make a case for anything in education, quote research and everyone will shut up.

"I would be most interested in seeing this research, sir."

"Yes, well, everybody should see it."

Mr. Reaf's eyes brightened. Now there's an idea. There's a way to show them.

"Yeah, that's not a bad idea," he said excitedly.

"What, sir?"

"I'm gonna dig up the research on grammar. I'm tired of everyone telling me what I should and shouldn't be doing in here. Yeah, that's it. Then, the next time somebody says to change what I'm doing, I'll just toss the research in his face."

"Please, sir, would you also make me a copy of this research?"

"Yeah, sure."

The sound of the door opening caught their attention. In crept the same group of kids as yesterday. They huddled just inside the door.

"Hey, Luis!" one of the girls called out to the janitor.

"Hello, my friends."

Luis, so that's the guy's name. Reaf saw his chance to escape. He stuffed his papers into his briefcase.

"Well, see you tomorrow," he said as he hurried around his desk.

"Have a wonderful evening, sir."

Looking over his shoulder, he paused at the door. "Same to you," he said facetiously.

The janitor grinned from ear to ear.

"Why not?"

Week One, Day Four

Kui, the one-legged dragon,
Is jealous of the centipede.
The centipede is jealous of the snake.
The snake is jealous of the wind.
The wind is jealous of the eye.
The eye is jealous of the mind.
Kui said to the centipede:
"I manage my one leg with difficulty:
How can you manage a hundred?"
The centipede replied:
"I do not manage them."

--*The Way of Chuang Tzu*
Thomas Merton

"Mr. Reaf, who is Kui?"

Reaf was late again. Mrs. Hurren had caught him in the hall, pestering him again about ordering those textbooks. Damn, she's a pain, he thought.

He hurried over to his desk, ignoring the question. Thank God he had Honors first period. Fifth or sixth would have dismantled the room by now.

"Who is Kui, Mr. Reaf?" a voice called out.

He set his briefcase on the desk, popped the latches on it simultaneously and reached in for his lesson-plan book.

"Settle down," he said automatically.

Then he noticed. He didn't hear a sound. Looking up from the desk, he saw twenty-five pairs of eyes, watching him. Suddenly he felt as if he'd been caught slurping spaghetti in a fancy restaurant. He nervously cleared his throat.

"Who is Kui, Mr. Reaf?" said the same voice in

exasperation. It was Mary, a quiet girl who sat in the back corner of the room.

"How should I know?" he responded. All heads turned back to Mary.

"Well, it's *your* quotation!" she threw back indignantly.

Mr. Reaf glanced quickly at the board. From the citation he guessed it was an Asian text, probably Chinese.

"That's an ancient Chinese quotation, Mary," he said, hoping his bluff would end her curiosity.

"Why is Kui jealous of everything?" she asked.

Boy, she wasn't letting go. Before he could think of an answer, Joanna jumped in.

"I think it's because she's unhappy."

"What's she unhappy about?" Mary yelled up the row to Joanna.

Joanna swung around.

"She's unhappy about having less than someone else."

"That's it!" called out Paul excitedly. "There *is* a pattern!"

"Pattern?" Reaf said.

"Kui has one leg, so he--"

"She!" interjected Joanna.

"He, she, big deal," Paul continued. "He's jealous of the centipede who has many legs. But the centipede is jealous of the snake because he--"

"She," interrupted Joanna again. Laughter filled the room.

"Okay, okay, *she* doesn't have to deal with legs. But the snake's jealous of the wind because she still has a body that she drags about, whereas the wind can move freely."

"So, great solver of riddles," called out Tom, a tall basketball player known for his cocky attitude. "Why's the wind jealous of the eye?"

Two hands shot up.

"Uh, yes, Brandon," Reaf said automatically.

"Because the wind and eye both move freely, but the wind cannot see," he said.

"Yeah, that's it!" yelled Paul. "And the eye is jealous of the mind because the mind can go anywhere."

"And it can see or imagine anything!" yelled Joanna.

Paul and Joanna gave each other a high-five slap with their hands.

"Well, that was very good, class," Reaf said. "You analyzed that very well. Now, if you'll turn to--"

"Mr. Reaf?" Mary called out again.

"Yes, Mary," he answered, with a little exasperation to let them know they couldn't go on with this.

"Why are people always jealous of each other? I mean, it seems people always want what somebody else has."

He stared at her blankly, surprised at the question.

"Yeah, Mr. Reaf," said Joanna. "If the mind is so free, why do people think about what they don't have?"

The class stared back at the teacher, waiting for an answer.

"Well, Mary, I guess people derive pleasure from owning things," Reaf said.

"What's wrong with wanting something that somebody else has?" called out Tom.

Suddenly Mr. Reaf remembered an old saying his grandfather had often repeated. *If you're always wanting more, you'll never have enough.*

"Well, Tom, perhaps this Chinese guy is saying that if you always want more, you never feel like you have enough."

"Yeah, I know what ya mean," yelled Joanna excitedly. "It's like 'shopping fever' at the mall. You know, like when your parents give you the charge cards and say you can only spend so much. Then, when you get there, you keep seeing more and more stuff you want. Pretty soon, like, you almost get dizzy because you don't know how you're going to get your hands on everything you want fast enough."

A number of heads nodded in agreement.

"Well, I think there is *one* thing that we could all get our hands on that would help us feel a lot better."

"What's that?" asked Tom excitedly.

"Your grammar book. Turn to page 42."

* * *

Mr. Reaf never got around to erasing the quote from the

board; consequently, he dealt with Kui the dragon all day long. Even a student in brain-dead third period asked him about it. Fifth period was quiet, since the gang of five had been suspended for a day. But sixth was in true form.

Hernandez hadn't been in the room a minute before he called out.

"Hey, Mr. Reaf? What's wrong with Kui's one leg? Has it gone limp on him?"

The class snickered at the sexual innuendo.

"Hernandez," Reaf said sternly, "the quote is about wanting what we can't have."

"That's what I'm talking about, Mr. Reaf. Kui ain't getting enough of what he wants. And if your leg ain't stiff, you ain't gonna get it."

The class laughed more loudly this time. Heads began to turn from Hernandez to the teacher.

Reaf decided it was time for a little humiliation. He stood up behind his desk.

"I think the quote is about insatiable desire, not insatiable chatter."

"That's just what I'm chattering about, Mr. Reaf. Some desires just don't go away."

Hernandez's response caught him off guard. Before he could attack again, Jose jumped in.

"How is it a centipede can move all those legs so fast, Mr. Reaf? Man, I see those things in my house all the time. They be running over you when you asleep."

There was a general shudder in the room.

"Hell, man, centipedes ain't nothing," boomed a voice from the back of the room. Every head turned around in surprise. The Johnson girl never said anything, at least anything that could be heard by a teacher. You felt her presence by her anger.

"My little sister woke up last week screaming her head off," she continued. "A damn cockroach had crawled in her mouth!"

Screams exploded throughout the room. Mr. Reaf shuddered at the image of those filthy, bristly legs and antennae creeping into a little girl's mouth.

"That's wrong, man. That's so wrong," shouted Jose. "Why they make us live in these stinking places. Where I stay at we got cockroaches everywhere."

Twenty different conversations ignited around the room. Insectomania was running rampant as sixth period shared war stories of living in the projects. Then, Johnson's angry voice could be heard over everyone's.

"And that white cracker landlord don't even live in the damn city!"

All heads turned toward Reaf. Suddenly, he was the enemy, the absentee landlord, the white general who sent out his army of rodents and roaches to drive these people into a rage. Mr. Reaf sat down and began straightening papers on his desk. Without looking up he said, "Ms. Johnson, have you considered calling an exterminator?"

Johnson rose to her feet. She was a big girl who towered over her classmates. The room was so quiet Reaf was sure he heard her knuckles pop as she clenched her fists.

"Mr. Reaf, I've considered being an exterminator!"

"I heard that!" a voice called out. A number of students chuckled, then grew quiet to see how the teacher would respond. Something told him if he mentioned grammar right now he was a dead man.

"Mr. Reaf?" It was Hernandez.

"Why you white people treat everybody so bad, man?"

"Yeah," said Jose. "You just like the dragon. You try to take everything."

"Now wait a minute," Mr. Reaf responded defensively. "I am not a landlord. I don't own your buildings. I don't even own my own place. I rent it. And I've got cockroaches, too. They were all over my breadbox yesterday morning."

"You got cockroaches, Mr. Reaf?" asked Hernandez incredulously.

"Yes, Hernandez, I do. I'm not proud of it, but I do." He turned to face him.

"Shoot, man, I thought cucarachas only liked dark meat."

Laughter exploded in the room. Mr. Reaf had been

watching the Johnson girl out of the corner of his eye. Grinning broadly, she sat back down.

"So, Mr. Reaf, what you gonna do about your cucarachas?" asked Juan.

"Well, what I should do is write a letter to the landlord."

"You best save that paper to squash bugs," Johnson called from the back of the room. Everyone laughed. Reaf smiled, then covered his mouth with his hand.

"Well, Ms. Johnson, I hear what you're saying, but it's the appropriate first step. If I'm going to file a complaint with the city, then they'll want to know if I've contacted the landlord about the problem first. And by writing a letter and dating it, I can keep a copy as a record."

"And what will the city do?" asked Juan. "It's run by the same white people that own the buildings."

Juan was probably right, thought Mr. Reaf. The rich don't care about these people, but he had to play the scenario out now.

"I'm not quite sure of the procedures, but I imagine they would eventually send out a health inspector. If the building didn't come up to code, the city could threaten the landlord with a fine."

"Man, the city isn't going to listen to you," Johnson yelled out angrily. "They just going to say you being filthy. They gonna blame the roaches on you."

"Then why not get the whole building to sign the letter?" called out Hernandez. "If everybody in the place complains together, then they can't blame one person."

"Yeah, like a petition," called out Jose.

Reaf stared at Hernandez in surprise. Since when had gang members become social activists?

"So why haven't you written *your* letter, Mr. Reaf?" asked Juan.

"Well, uh . . . I guess I've just been lazy. But it's not a bad idea. Why don't we all write that letter. Let's tell these landlords how we feel."

It was a gamble to return the class to his control. Either they would go for the idea, or he'd lose them. A loud slap made everyone jump.

"Sorry, Mr. Reaf," called out Johnson. "A cockroach ran out of my notebook." She paused, then asked with a grin, "So what we gonna say in this here letter?"

He looked at Johnson. She was eyeing him impishly as she ripped a sheet of paper out of her spiral notebook. He had to smile. Students began asking each other for paper and pen.

"Well, okay. This is a business letter. So let's begin this way." He jumped out of his seat and hurried to the blackboard to find a scrap of yellow chalk.

"Again, we need to date the letter so we can prove when we first notified the landlord, so put your address and the date centered at the top of your paper. Here, I'll put a model on the board for you."

* * *

Thirty minutes later Mr. Reaf sat at his desk in a daze. On top were piled twenty-four letters of complaint. He couldn't believe his eyes, or his hands. Five dust-covered fingers were extended on his right hand. How in God's name?

The metal door groaned.

"Good afternoon, sir."

Pedro, or Luis, as the students called him, stood inside the door, smiling. "I trust you had a pleasant day," he said, leaning against the broom handle as if it were a microphone for a standup comic.

"I had a very good day, thank you," Reaf said, leaning back in his chair. "Yes, I had a very good day. We really accomplished some things in here today."

"And how did you manage your students so well today, sir?" Luis asked as he began his rhythmic sweeping down the far aisle.

Mr. Reaf didn't answer immediately. How did I manage them? he asked himself. Why did it seem to go so much more easily today? He couldn't remember calling anyone down all day. He stared at the empty seats. Johnson's desk in the back. Hernandez's in the far corner under the blackboard. He smiled. Yes, Hernandez, cucarachas like white meat too. Above Hernandez's desk he noticed the Debate Club's quotation.

"I do not manage them," he read slowly.

"Sorry, sir, I did not hear you."

"I said I didn't manage them."

"Ah--" another one of those long, all-knowing *ah's*. Who did this guy think he was? One of the three wise men?

The rhythmic sweeping began again. Luis moved to the back row. Mr. Reaf felt a wave of exhaustion pass through him. He put his feet up on the desk and closed his eyes. A few minutes passed as he began to doze off.

"And, Mr. Reaf, what will you teach tomorrow, if I may ask?" Mr. Reaf jumped in his seat.

"Huh? Oh, tomorrow, well tomorrow is Friday, the fifth," he said, picking up his lesson-plan book. "I usually show a video or film on Friday. It's a little trick I've learned from years of experience. These kids would rather stare at a screen any day than do any real work. So I get a film for Friday and hold it over them all week. Based on their score for the week, they either get to see the film or do seatwork."

"Their score, sir? How do you give a class a score?" Luis asked while sweeping up an aisle toward Reaf's desk.

"Oh, it's part of my system. If they've failed me more than twice a week, they don't get to see the film."

"Failed you, sir?"

"Yes, not done the work, or misbehaved. If they cause too much trouble, they don't deserve to see the film."

"And who will not see the film this week?"

Reaf put his hands behind his head and stretched back, thinking out loud. "Well, I guess fifth and sixth periods. They've been pretty bad all week, and a I need to set an example with them. They need to learn the consequences of their actions."

He felt his stomach tighten as he pictured the fights ahead. It had to be done, though. He must let them know who was in control. He picked up sixth period's cockroach letters and tossed them in his briefcase.

Suddenly the door groaned and in stormed the debaters. Reaf pulled his feet off the desk.

"Hello, Luis!" sang out a number of the kids.

"Hello, my friends," he answered.

The teacher folded the other classes' grammar exercises lengthwise, stretched a rubber band over them, and let it snap with a loud pop. Stuffing the papers into his briefcase, he rose and headed for the door.

"Well, I'm off. Don't you kids wreck the room."

"Goodbye, sir," answered Luis, who was now surrounded by the Debate Club. "Have a nice evening."

"Sure, you too," Reaf mumbled without looking back.

"Why not?" the janitor called out.

Week One, Day Five

You often say, "I would give, but only to the deserving."
The trees in your orchard say not so, nor the flocks in your pasture.
They give that they may live, for to withhold is to perish.
Surely he who is worthy to receive his days
and his nights is worthy of all else from you.
And he who has deserved to drink from the ocean of life
deserves to fill his cup from your little stream.

--*The Prophet*
Kahlil Gibran

"Okay, first period, settle down. As I've mentioned before, if you've worked hard all week, you get to see a film on Friday. This film is in two parts, and each part lasts forty-five minutes, so we must begin immediately. It's called *I Will Fight No More Forever*, and it's the true story of an Indian chief who led his people on an amazing journey while trying to evade the U.S. Cavalry. I don't want to tell you any more because I don't want to ruin it for you. Mary, would you get the lights?"

"But, Mr. Reaf," called out Paul, "are we going to discuss the quote for today?"

Reaf glanced quickly at the board.

"Okay, yes, well . . . you're deserving, and that's what the quote's about, so let's see the film. Hit the lights, Mary."

Film days were usually winners. Second and third periods loved the first part of the story as much as Honors did. Reaf even showed it to Study Hall since they had been good all week, too. Then fifth period arrived.

"Hey, Mr. Reaf, I hear you got a cool flick today!" called out Jackson, one of Ellis's buddies on the volleyball team. She swaggered up to his desk, grinning from ear to ear.

"Yes, Ms. Jackson. I do have a good film today. It's about the unfair treatment of a group of people in this country." He looked at her coolly as he spoke.

"I hear that!" she said loudly, turning to her classmates.

"Now if you'll all take your seats and turn to page 38 in your grammar texts, we'll get started."

"What?" Jackson yelled as she swung around to face the teacher.

Angry objections pelted him from around the room. "What about our movie, man?" "You said we'd see a movie."

"Fifth period, quiet down!" he yelled over the din. "In my classes you get to see the movie if you've earned it. This week I have had to call you down again and again. I have even had to throw a few of you out of the room." Mr. Reaf stared at Jackson, Ellis, and the other three girls as he threw out this last little barb.

"When you learn to do your work in here, then you will deserve to see the movie. Perhaps next week you will see the first part. Now let's get started. Mr. Davis, begin by reading the definition of a noun at the top of page 38."

"That's cold, man," yelled out Jackson as she plopped down in her seat.

"*Cold* is an adjective, Ms. Jackson. You must be on the wrong page. Or perhaps you don't care if the class sees the movie next week."

Jackson shook her head and mumbled a few curse words. The entire class began to grumble. He knew he had to get them started or he would be fighting them all period.

"Mr. Davis, read from the top, please."

" 'You often say, "I would give, but only to the deserving," ' " Davis read slowly.

"Wait a minute, Mr. Davis. What are you reading? We're on page 38."

"I reading what's on the board. Ain't we suppose to start with that?"

All heads turned to the board. Reaf watched them plod through the words, lips silently searching for meaning.

"Yes, we normally begin with the quotation, but--"
"Mr. Reaf!" interrupted Ellis.
"What, Ms. Ellis?" he said with exasperation.
"How can you write that on the board and then treat us like you do? That ain't fair!"

Oh God, he thought. Here we go with the age-old complaint of the poor and stupid: Life isn't fair. He'd heard it a million times. Well, he had plenty of ammo to shoot that argument down.

"That's right, Ms. Ellis. Life isn't fair. Who ever told you it was, anyway? In fact, our very economic structure is built on the idea that some will have and others will not. If you look--"

"Wait a minute, man," interrupted Ellis again. "You ain't got to tell us life isn't fair. I live that crap every day. I'm talking about your quote. It says you should give to people whether you think they be deserving or not. It don't say nothing about life being fair."

"Well, I'm not sure I believe that."

"Then why you write it on the board?" yelled out Jackson. "You a damn hypocrite."

Mr. Reaf rose behind his desk. "Watch your language, Mr. Jackson, if you want to stay in here."

"Why would anyone want to stay in this tired classroom?" called out Ellis.

Ellis's attack opened a barrage of animosity. Reaf fought against the growing tide of noise and anger, but he knew they were determined to drown him out. He'd witnessed the cruelty of these kids often. Normally they turned their anger and frustration on each other. In fact, he often used their rivalries as a source of control. But heaven help him on those rare instances when they banded together. They became sharks on a feeding frenzy.

By the time the bell rang, four kids had been sent to the office, and Reaf was left floating in the debris of hurt feelings and resentment that had once been a classroom. News spreads fast in schools. As sixth period took their seats, a number of students looked up to read the quote, then eyed Mr. Reaf suspiciously. By their hushed comments to each other, he could tell they were ready for a fight. Reaf sat at his desk, staring down at fifth period's papers. Not one was completed. He knew he couldn't go through another fifth period.

"Mr. Reaf?" It was Juan. "You grade our letters?"

Letters? Damn! He'd completely forgotten about their letters.

"Sorry, Juan. I didn't get to them," he said, looking up. In fact, he hadn't even taken them from his briefcase. A few moans rippled across the room.

"I promise to have them on Monday."

"Mr. Reaf?" called out Hernandez. "Why didn't you grade them, man? Don't we deserve some of your attention?"

Before Reaf could respond to this unexpected attack, Johnson called out.

"Hey, Mr. Reaf, why don't you grade them while we watch the movie?"

Reaf stared at her, wide-eyed. She had him and she knew it. To refuse would mean all-out war. He couldn't bear it. It was Friday, and he only had to survive one more period. He let out the breath he didn't realize he'd been holding.

"I guess that's a good idea, Ms. Johnson," he said. "Jose, will you get the lights, please."

The lights went out to a couple of high-five slaps among the victors. Who cares, thought Reaf. Reaching in his briefcase, he found the stack of letters. He yanked the rubber band, and they sprang open in his hand. Looking up to make sure everyone was watching the movie, he began reading the first letter.

September 4

Dear Mr. Landlord:
You stink man. You make my family live in filthe houses . . .

Reaf realized he couldn't bear to read these now. He put them away and reached for fifth period's worksheets. Now here was something he could sink his teeth into. When he handed them back covered in red ink on Monday, they'd see the price of their disrespect.

The teacher jumped when the bell rang forty minutes later. Setting the stack of letters down, he made a quick scan of the room to see what was going on. Everyone was still staring at the screen as the first part came to an end. These kids were really into this movie. When "End of Part 1" rolled across the screen, the kids sprang like jackrabbits out of their seats for the door. Poor Luis was caught in the rush. He had just leaned on the door when the first kid pulled it open, catapulting Luis into the room. Hernandez caught him.

"You okay, Luis?" asked Hernandez.

"I'm fine, Carlos. I just didn't expect to find any students in here after the bell."

"Yeah, well, we're outta here. Bye, Mr. Reaf," called out Hernandez.

Mr. Reaf looked up, surprised. A few other students called good-bye as they hurried out the door.

"Well, sir," said Luis once everyone had left, "you seemed to have 'not managed them' again very well."

"Some I managed, some I didn't," Reaf responded as he began to straighten his desk.

"You had troubles, sir?" Luis asked as he shuffled to the back of the room.

Sitting down, Reaf quickly ran through his finger count. Four to one.

"Yes, fifth period acted a bit childishly."

"And why is that, sir?" Luis asked as he began to sweep between rows in the back of the room.

"Oh, like most kids, they want rewards even if they haven't earned them."

"And you refused them then?" he asked, looking up.

"Of course," he said.

"I imagine that caused some pain."

The word *pain* brought back the intensity of the attack during fifth. The "hypocrite" wound was still fresh. Without answering, Reaf began gathering fifth period's papers together.

Luis continued his rhythmic sweeping. Mr. Reaf moved stuff around on his desk, wanting to leave. Something seemed to be holding him there, though. He tried to remember any plans he had made for the weekend. Instinctively he reached for his lesson-plan book, then laughed to himself. There was nothing in there to get him through the weekend. Suddenly he felt very sad. What kind of life was this? Here was the weekend, and he had nothing to look forward to.

"Mr. Reaf, did you find that research on grammar you were looking for?"

Reaf looked up and smiled. Yes, that's it, he thought. I *do* have something to do this weekend.

"Not yet," he said excitedly. "That is something I plan to do this weekend. You see, I live near the university, so it is easy for me to do a quick computer search at the library."

"How do these computer searches work, sir?"

"Well, it's really amazing. You just type in a few key words, or descriptors, as they call them. Then the computer searches its memory for any studies having these terms in the titles."

"I think this computer search sounds like a very good thing."

"Well, it is remarkably fast. The computer completes the entire search in a matter of seconds."

"Yes, I'm sure the speed is helpful, but I think it is good for another reason. Being a machine, the computer is rather open-minded."

"What?" Reaf said incredulously. Luis stepped toward his desk.

"It is my experience, sir, that when humans search for something, they often see only what they want to see. This computer will see everything, will it not?"

"Yes, but then a human must sift through the research. So if your theory holds, then a human could still draw out only the data that proves his point."

"True," said Luis nodding, "but as my ancestors have said, 'It is harder to ignore the mosquito once he's under the netting.' "

Mr. Reaf cocked his head sideways and stared at the

janitor. Who is this guy? he thought. And where does he get these stupid sayings? Standing there in that same white shirt, black pants, and tan vest. Does he ever change his clothes? At least he doesn't smell. Suddenly he realized the janitor was staring right back at him.

The creak of rusty hinges caused them both to look toward the door. In poured the debaters.

"Hello, Luis," they called out.

"Hello, my friends," he responded cheerfully. Reaf saw his cue to exit.

"Well, it's Friday, and I'm outta here." He grabbed his briefcase and headed for the door.

"Good luck with the mosquitoes, sir."

"What?" Reaf said, turning around. Luis smiled. "Oh, yeah, the research. Thanks. Have a good day."

"Why not?" the janitor replied as the door slammed shut.

The Weekend

In college Mr. Reaf had had a professor who used to say, "Always expect the unexpected." Reaf liked such sayings that sounded so right, so profound that one never stopped to consider the depth of their meaning. To Reaf, such phrases were a warm teddy bear to cuddle up to in times of doubt or trouble. He heard them in the soft bass voice of a father who picked him up when he fell, or in the soothing lilt of his mother's whispers as she tucked him under just-laundered sheets. He felt assured that there was someone wiser and in control, someone who could explain life's profoundness in its simplest terms. Such words remain comforting to us all until something happens to wake us up, to alter the way our inner child sees the world. From that moment on, we begin to test those words against our own experience. They no longer possess their comforting ring. Instead, they render a disquieting alarm that life is more than we've allowed ourselves to see.

Reaf left for the university early Saturday morning. He was a man with a mission, heading into known territory. He had always loved doing library research. Once in a college paper he described the research process as a vine blooming from spring to summer. From one small shoot, technological tendrils reached out through furrows of dark stacks, bearing buds of ideas and finally spreading before you in a garden ripe with knowledge. Reaf thought it was a pretty good metaphor even if the professor didn't.

His computer search of "grammar" and "writing" produced over a hundred studies. As they began to roll across the screen, he scanned the titles, looking for anything to support his belief that teaching grammar improved writing, thinking, language ability, and logical reasoning. Once and for all he would silence those who criticized his curriculum.

It dawned on him that with so many studies completed over the years, he might find a journal article that summarized most of the research. Surely some poor grad student had been forced to read and abstract all this research. And, he imagined, some professor probably got first billing for all the work.

After only a few minutes of scanning the computer's memory, Reaf found three summaries of research that looked relevant to his cause. Copying down the microfiche numbers, he hurried down to the microfilm room. Twenty minutes later he held photocopies of all three studies. Finding an old study carrel in a dimly lit lower level in the stacks, he set his briefcase down, leaned back in his chair, and plopped his feet on the desk. Pulling out the first study, he began to read. He would remain in that position for the next hour. To any observer the teacher would seem a stable presence quietly strengthening his intellectual underpinnings, tending his mental garden. No one could have detected that a large part of his essence was wilting away. No one would have ever imagined that the man sitting in the corner was committing intellectual suicide.

The first article provided an explanation of how grammar had come to hold such a sacred place in our school culture. It seemed that in the 1800s, the Industrial Revolution created a new class of people in England--the middle class. In a country where status was determined by bloodlines, however, these new rich had little social prestige. Consequently, many members of this class chose language for asserting their power and prestige. The new middle class began creating a complex system of rules for speaking and writing that only they were privy to.

Because Greek and Latin represented classic purity and divine inspiration, these languages were chosen as models. Unfortunately, these languages are Romance languages and possess very different rules of syntax from English, which is of Germanic derivation. Naturally, inconsistencies and exceptions to rules began to appear.

Creating new grammatical rules became an interesting

pastime for some. The rules themselves could be extremely subjective. For example, Johannis Willis felt a distinction between *shall* and *will* would improve the language. Thus he created the "I shall"-but-"you will" rule. Mr. Willis was a mathematician by trade.

More important, the function of grammar itself changed during the nineteenth century. Grammar is a description of how a language works. Because language is always evolving, grammar ought to reflect and explain those changes. In the nineteenth century, grammar became prescriptive rather than descriptive. Rules were created to ensure that "proper" language did not change over time.

Well, Reaf thought, right or wrong, grammar had dictated the way people should talk for two centuries now, and it was his duty to teach kids those rules so that they could function in society. If kids did not know the rules, then they could not apply them to their speaking and writing. And the only way to teach grammar was to practice, practice, practice.

He tossed aside the historical article and picked up the first review of the research. The first study described was carried out in 1903. The researcher found that many students who had a good comprehension of grammar still wrote compositions of inferior quality. Well, that was true once in a while, he thought. He did have Honors students who got A's on mechanics and C's on content. They could tell him grammatically what every word was in each sentence and why every comma was in its place, but their compositions were often simple and full of cliches.

In 1906 another researcher looked at the carry over of elementary grammar training to high school composition. He found no significant correlation between the two. In 1936 the Curriculum Commission of the National Council of Teachers of English reviewed the previous thirty years' worth of research regarding grammar and composition. They concluded that most grammar instruction should be stopped, since attempts at proving a knowledge of grammar was useful had failed.

By 1950 the *Encyclopedia of Educational Research* had

stated that the study of grammar didn't help students interpret literature, didn't discipline the mind, didn't help students acquire a foreign language, didn't improve reading skills or language behavior, and didn't improve writing. The report also called sentence diagramming a meaningless activity since one must already know the rules in order to perform the task. Research in the sixties, seventies, and eighties echoed those findings.

Mr. Reaf's mind began to go into a tailspin. He shut his eyes and rubbed his temples. He felt light headed and nauseated. He picked up the review and tossed it aside, then he stared down at his hands in his lap. His hands! God, he hadn't noticed how bad they looked. The skin was dry and cracked. Yellow chalk dust glared from under the fingernails. The hangnail on his right middle finger had become red and sore. Why haven't I put a Band-aid on it, he thought. Why haven't I taken care of my hands?

Reaching in his back pocket, he yanked out a handkerchief and began to dig feverishly at the chalk dust. He moved from one nail to the next, wetting the handkerchief in his mouth and shoving it under each nail. But the nails were stained, and no matter how hard he dug, most of the yellow remained. Frustrated, he stuffed the handkerchief back into his pocket. Reaf looked up to see a college student staring at him from across the room. Embarrassed, he pulled his feet off the desk and grabbed the third research study, but after a few sentences, he couldn't bear to read anymore. He lowered his head on the desk, reached up with a trembling hand, and switched off the light.

Week Two, Day One

If by forsaking a small pleasure one finds a great joy, he who is wise will look to the greater and leave what is less.

--The Dhammapada

"Mr. Reaf. Mr. Reaf! . . . Excuse me, Mr. Reaf."

Someone was tugging on his right elbow as he pushed through the crowded main hallway toward the teacher's lounge.

"Mr. Reaf?"

Turning, he faced Mrs. Hurren.

"Sorry to hold you up, Mr. Reaf. I just needed to tell you a few things."

He stared blankly at her. She always seems so earnest, he thought.

"First," she continued as they were jostled by kids scurrying and screaming to each other, "be sure to get the order for the new books in by next Monday. And second, I'm afraid you will not be able to use the VCR for your film this Friday. We have a guest speaker coming, and she needs it. I've checked the sign-up sheet in the library, and the only day it's available is Wednesday, so I've signed you up for then. I hope that is okay, Mr. Reaf?"

Mrs. Hurren paused and looked at him questioningly. "Mr. Reaf, did you hear me?"

"Yes, Mrs. Hurren."

"Is that okay about the VCR then?"

"That's fine, Mrs. Hurren," he said, looking down the hallway.

She stared at him with concern. "Mr. Reaf, are you feeling okay? You look a bit pale."

He turned back to face her and suddenly became aware of her appearance. She stood before him in a lavender skirt and a white blouse. A matching lavender bow was tied smartly around her collar. A wave of auburn hair kept falling into her eyes like an autumn leaf flapping in the wind. Brushing the hair back from her eyes, she peered at him earnestly. I don't want your pity, he thought.

"Mr. Reaf?"

"Sorry, Mrs. Hurren. It's Monday, and I'm a bit foggy. Don't worry. I shall . . . uh, will get your book order in."

He could hear first period from outside the quonset hut as he pushed against the heavy metal door. It sounded like a crowded truck-stop restaurant in there. How could he face these kids today? What did he have to teach them? He headed straight for his desk for refuge.

He set his briefcase on his desk, but it tipped over and fell with a loud slap. Heads turned in his direction, and the class grew quiet. Feeling their eyes on him, he opened the briefcase. On top of the stacks of papers lay his lesson-plan book. He stared at it, then sat down, hiding behind the opened briefcase.

Soon nervous whispers rippled through the classroom. Looking up to see who was talking, he noticed a student turn to look at the blackboard. There in the right-hand corner was the Debate Club's quote.

"Mr. Reaf?" It was Paul.

"Yes."

"We've been talking about today's quote. Everybody seems to have a different interpretation."

Reaf looked down at his lesson-plan book.

"Mr. Reaf?" said Paul. His teenage voice cracked with concern.

"Yes, Paul."

"What do *you* think the quote means?"

He peered over the briefcase at the board. What do I think? Reaf read the quote. *If by forsaking a small pleasure one finds a great joy, he who is wise will look to the greater and leave what is less.*

"I guess it's talking about sacrifice, Paul," he said half-heartedly.

"That's what I said, Mr. Reaf," Joanna said excitedly. "I said it meant a girl shouldn't sacrifice herself to a boy who wants to have sex with her."

There was a loud gasp from a number of students in the room, followed by embarrassed giggles. No one ever talked about sex in his classes. Reaf stared wide-eyed at Joanna.

"It's the same thing my granddaddy told me," she continued. "He lives on a farm in North Carolina."

The teacher's curiosity was aroused now. He straightened up and asked, "What did your grandfather say, Joanna?"

"Well, you'll probably laugh, but he says, 'Kill a calf, you only get veal. Kill a cow, you get meal upon meal.' " Laughter erupted in the room.

"What!?" yelled Tom from across the room. "We're talking about sex here, not steaks."

Joanna winced, then looked at her teacher.

"Wait a minute, now. Quiet down. Perhaps Joanna would like to explain further."

"Well, Mr. Reaf, I know everyone thinks you're a prude if you don't have sex with a guy in high school, but I believe that sex can be something really special and you should wait till you're with a person you really love."

"Well, what's wrong with having both?" called out Tom. "I like ribs and I like veal too." A number of boys laughed loudly. Tom was a handsome, black-haired, blue-eyed boy who usually had a girl on his arm wherever he walked on campus. As a starter on the basketball team, he commanded a lot of respect from other students.

"Why can't you have the small pleasures and the greater joys?" he continued. Mr. Reaf realized that Tom was not kidding. He had asked his question with great sincerity. "I mean, why does it always seem to be a choice of either/or in life?"

"You're missing the point," called Rachel from the back row. "If you take the calf, there's no cow left. If you submit to small pleasures, then the greater ones lose their meaning."

"What meaning?" asked Tom. "We're talking about sex here?"

"Maybe you're talking about sex," responded Joanna, "but I'm talking about sharing something very special with someone you've spent a lot of time with, with someone you've come to care about in spite of his shortcomings, with someone you have invested a lot of time in."

"Yeah," said Rachel. "Finding sex is easy. Finding love takes time."

"And sacrifice," Mr. Reaf blurted out.

Every head in the room jerked in his direction. He ducked back behind the top of the briefcase. Surprised, the class waited for more. They knew he was divorced. And they knew he never shared his personal life with them in any way. The silence closed in on him as quickly as Christmas shoppers fill an elevator.

Peering back over the briefcase, Reaf said defensively, "Well, you asked what I thought the quote meant."

The class continued to stare, silent, wanting more. He looked down at his hands, which suddenly felt clammy.

"I just think love means making some sacrifices. You can't have everything. I know some of you probably think you can." Mr. Reaf looked back up at Tom.

"I thought I could have just about anything I wanted when I was your age. I wanted all the small pleasures and the great joy. I realize now I was just selfish." He stared down at his open briefcase. He could still see the pain in his wife's face when she confronted him about the affair. He looked back up at the class.

"In my opinion the quote is saying that if you're forever putting your energy into fulfilling small pleasures, into immediate gratification, you're not building the foundations that real love requires. I guess you're only kidding yourself." He let the briefcase lid fall shut.

The class stared at him, dumbfounded.

* * *

The conversation about sacrifice continued the rest of the period, in fact, the rest of the day. Mr. Reaf had second and third periods write what they thought the quote meant. Fifth came in saying that they had heard his class was pretty cool today. The gang of five talked about their experiences on the volleyball team. Carlson said their coach talked about the same thing. Team members should sacrifice an easy shot whenever they could set a teammate for a sure spike.

Near the end of class someone asked what the Dhammapada was. Mr. Reaf realized that all day long he and his students had talked about these words without even understanding the source. Fifth period looked surprised when he said he didn't know.

"I'll go to the library and look it up," shouted the Macy girl, one of the gang of five.

Reaf hesitated. He had never trusted this girl. She sat in the back making comments to her neighbors and giving him looks that would drop a sparrow in mid flight. The class watched him, knowing what he was thinking.

"Well, do you want me to go or not?" she asked brusquely.

"Yes, but please hurry, Ms. Macy. The class would like to know before the period ends." Macy jumped up and headed for the door.

"Yeah," yelled Carlson. "Don't take any small pleasures in the ladies room while we're sitting here waiting for our greater joy."

Everyone burst out laughing.

"That was great, Carlson," Reaf said, laughing.

"Thanks, Mr. Reaf," she said, grinning from ear to ear. Their eyes met and held for a moment, reflecting, perhaps for the first time, something other than contempt.

Sixth period entered excitedly. The word had obviously gotten out that no grammar was done in Mr. Reaf's class today.

"Hey, Mr. Reaf. You grade our letter?" called out Juan.

Damn! Reaf slapped the desk with his hand. He had completely forgotten about their letters.

"I'm sorry, Juan. I swear to you I'll grade them tonight."

"Mr. Reaf, by the time you get those letters graded, my brother and sister will be carried away by cockroaches," called out Johnson, grinning impishly.

Reaf smiled. "Sorry, Ms. Johnson, I promise I will have them tomorrow."

"Hey, Mr. Reaf, tell the truth, man," said Hernandez. "You didn't grade them because, like those Dampuda people, you were enjoying too many small pleasures."

Surprised, he looked at Hernandez.

"The Dhammapada, Mr. Hernandez, is not a group of people. It is a collection of sayings compiled somewhere around the third century before Christ that suggests a right path of living for Buddhists. (Thank you, Ms. Macy.) And I can say in all honesty, Mr. Hernandez, that I did not have any small pleasures this weekend."

"That's too bad, man," called out the Sanford boy from the back corner. "I scored a number of small pleasures this weekend."

Everyone in the class turned to stare at Sanford, who was slouched down in his desk, grinning broadly while picking his teeth with a toothpick. It was common knowledge that he dealt drugs and was a gang member, or "banger," as they called each other. His gang was called the Sharks. But in school he usually had sense enough not to draw attention to himself. When Reaf noticed how red his eyes were, he understood his cocky attitude.

"And how much greater joy did you bring anybody else, Sanford?" Hernandez suddenly yelled.

Sanford sat up to see who had attacked him. He spotted Hernandez. The animosity between the two was electric. The room began to sizzle with anger.

"Who you kidding, Hernandez?" Sanford shot back. "You know no white man gonna let you have any joy in this world. But I got me a lady and some stuff this weekend, and for niggers it don't get any better than that."

"How would you know if you always high? You so messed up all the time you already decided your future!" shouted Hernandez. The heads in the room turned from one to the other.

"What future? I ain't talking about future. Man, you better wake up. You think the white folks is gonna let you have a future. Why you think they keep you in the ghetto, brother? You think they preparing you for some management position there? The best you gonna get is a blue coat at McDonald's. Is that a large or small fries, Ma'am?" Sanford said mockingly. A number of students laughed.

"Gentlemen, I'm sure--"

"You wrong!" Hernandez jumped in. "You think I'm being used, but every time you buy stuff you just increasing their power over your butt."

"Yeah, well at least my butt is smiling. And when my ass gets gunned down I'll have had some pleasures . . . like your sister."

Hernandez leapt to his feet, fists clenched.

"Mr. Hernandez! Sit down!" Reaf yelled immediately. "Sanford, you may excuse yourself from the room."

"For what, man?" Sanford yelled.

"For using drugs in school."

"You got no proof."

"Then you can leave for cursing in my room."

"Fuck you, man," Sanford said. He leapt to his feet, knocking his desk over. Then he strutted out of the room, pointing his finger at Hernandez as he passed him.

Hernandez remained standing until the door slammed shut.

Mr. Reaf took a deep breath. "Okay, class--"

Suddenly four bells sounded. The intercom blared loudly, "THIS IS A FIRE DRILL. PLEASE FOLLOW YOUR TEACHER TO THE DESIGNATED STAGING AREA IN A QUIET AND ORDERLY MANNER." Oh God, thought Reaf, Sanford couldn't have set the school on fire that quickly. The class jumped up from their seats, talking loudly.

"Okay, let's go," yelled Reaf over the noise. "Jackson, please shut the windows."

Jackson headed for the door, as did a number of other students.

"Whoa!" Reaf yelled. The door slammed shut as Jackson

and a few others made their escape. The students still in the room paused to look at their teacher. "Now, the rest of you follow me out to the blacktop. And try to stay together."

Mr. Reaf led the way out the door. Just as well, he thought. God knows what I would have done with them next.

* * *

The classes stayed outside till the end of the period. The kids then headed over to the bus-loading area. Mr. Reaf walked back to the quonset hut and threw his weight against the door. Both he and the door groaned in unison.

"Good afternoon, Mr. Reaf!"

The teacher jumped.

"God, Ped--, uh Luis, you scared me half to death."

"Very sorry, sir," he said as he picked up paper in the back of the room.

Reaf plopped down in the seat behind his desk, letting out a grunt as he hit the seat.

"Excuse me, Mr. Reaf?"

Reaf looked at the janitor.

"Were you able to do your research last weekend?"

Damn, not that, not now.

"Yes," Reaf mumbled as he began to toss papers into his briefcase. Luis started sweeping.

"And what did you find, sir?"

He stared down at his hands, yellowed and cracked. He was beginning to wonder if the skin wasn't permanently stained.

What did I find, he thought. Oh, nothing much--just that what I've been doing for fifteen years is wrong.

Luis had stopped sweeping. He stood at the back of the room, those dark brown eyes watching Reaf intently. The teacher looked up and their eyes met. Suddenly he didn't care anymore. Who was this janitor going to tell, anyway? What did he care what this little man thought. The words began to come out mechanically, like a serial killer's confession.

"The research says there's no transfer from isolated grammar skills to one's writing. In other words, teaching grammar the way I do doesn't improve writing, nor does it improve language ability, since there is little transfer to usage either. Furthermore, sentence diagramming, which is supposed to teach the parts of speech, is a meaningless activity, since one must know the parts of speech before doing it."

"Are you saying that it is wrong to teach grammar, sir?"

Mr. Reaf slammed his briefcase shut.

"No! I am saying that how I teach it is wrong."

Luis leaned against his broom. "What will you do, Mr. Reaf?"

He looked down at his desk. The lesson-plan book lay there, still closed from this morning. A thin film of chalk dust had settled on top of it. He traced a triangle in the dust with one finger.

"I feel like my life is becoming a disaster," he mumbled, then raised his eyes. Luis stood in the back of the room with a silly grin on his face.

"What the hell are you smiling at?"

"Excuse me, sir. Please do not think I am laughing at you. It is just that when I hear the word *disaster*, I am reminded of something about the Chinese people."

"What?" Reaf asked angrily.

"Well, sir, the Chinese word for disaster is also their word for opportunity.

Reaf leaned back in his chair. "Oh, so I'm supposed to see this as an opportunity. To do what? To change?"

The janitor just stared at him.

"Well, I don't plan to, I can't, anyway." He paused, then said softly, "I just can't."

"Why, sir?"

A lump rose in Mr. Reaf's throat. His chest felt heavy. He had to move. Rising from his desk, he crossed the room to one of the small windows along the wall. He grabbed the two metal rods at the bottom of the glass and pushed them outward. The window opened with a loud squeal. Outside on the grass in front of the chainlink fence that surrounded the school, he could see a boy and girl laughing and wrestling playfully. He could also feel Luis waiting for his answer. Without turning around, he forced the next words out.

"Don't you see? If I change, it means I'm admitting I've been wrong. If I change, it means that for fifteen years I've been wasting kids' lives. And I didn't want to do that. I fought hard to teach them something that I thought would help them. Now, suddenly, I'm told that if anything, I held them back. I can't live with that. I have to go on just as before, as if nothing has happened."

"But Mr. Reaf, it seems to me you don't have to stop teaching grammar, just how you teach it."

"I can't," he said, still looking out the window.

"Why, sir?"

Reaf turned to face Luis and said resolutely, "I don't know how to teach differently. I can't change now. I have my system."

Luis didn't answer. He stared at Mr. Reaf with those big doe eyes of his. The silence closed. A wave of sadness broke across the teacher. Reaf leaned against the wall, feeling drained. How much longer could he feel so bad about his life?

"Mr. Reaf, have you ever heard of Famous Amos?"

Looking up, he saw a grin spread slowly across Luis's face. The teacher straightened up. "What? The cookie man? What are you talking about?"

"Yes, Mr. Reaf, the cookie man. You may not know this, but he was struggling in New York to make a living for his wife and family before he became a millionaire. Everyone said he would never make it when he decided to market his homemade cookies. But Mr. Amos had a very different attitude that might apply here."

"Is it his secret to making dough?" the teacher quipped.

Luis laughed. "That's very good, sir. I am glad to see you haven't lost your sense of humor. And in a way, it is his secret for making dough. Amos said, "If you really want to change your life, count the number of times you've said, 'I will,' then count the number of times you've said, 'I can't.' If you're not where you want to be, chances are you've said, 'I can't' more times than you've said, 'I will.' "

Reaf stared at the small man, who stood smiling at him, a sparkle in his eyes.

"Well, that sounds nice, but I can say, 'I will' all I want to and I still won't know what to do tomorrow." He turned back to the window. "Don't you see, I don't know any other way to teach."

"Are you saying you can't, Mr. Reaf, or you won't?"

"I don't know what to do, damn it!" Reaf turned and yelled.

"But didn't the research also tell you what to do?"

"Yeah, well. It talked about teaching grammar in the context of student writing. But these kids don't know how to write. They never write in here. What could they possibly have to say? They don't have anything to talk about. They just bitch and complain. They don't . . ."

Suddenly sixth period's letters popped into his mind. He rushed over to the desk and spun the briefcase around. Clicking the locks, he opened the briefcase and rummaged feverishly through the stacks of grammar worksheets. God, where were they? Did he toss them out? Damn! . . . Then on the bottom he found a stack with a big 6 scribbled on the outside paper. He peeked inside. It was the letters.

Luis had turned to watch him. "Find what you were looking for, sir?"

"Yes, I guess I did have one class do some writing."

"Well then, sir, that's a start."

"Yeah, a start, but what about Wednesday, what do I do then?" he said defensively, tossing the papers back into the briefcase.

"Well, you can show the other part of your film about Chief Joseph on Wednesday."

Surprised, he looked up at Luis. "How did you know I was showing a film?"

"Because sir, I check the schedule in the media center each afternoon in order to set up the VCR for the next day."

"Well, that's efficient of you," Reaf said sarcastically. "Then why don't you sneak it down to my room on Friday, where it's supposed to be. Damn, I hate it when they mess up my schedule. I always save the film for last."

"Do you have to save it for last, sir?"

"Yes, it's one of my rules. Always save the best for last. Whether it's food, clothing, or whatever, I save it for last to savor it, to have something to look forward to."

Reaf slammed his briefcase shut and hurried around the desk to leave. "Mr. Reaf?"

"What?" he said impatiently. He didn't want to hear any more weird stuff from this guy.

Luis turned to face him. Pulling the door open, Reaf looked back at him.

"You want to be getting home, Mr. Reaf. I will tell you another time perhaps."

"No, no. Go on. Just make it quick," the teacher said guiltily. Luis smiled.

"Well, there is an old Jewish story of a young man who was eating grapes when his rabbi made a call. He noticed that the rabbi was watching him intently as he ate during their talk. 'Rabbi,' he said, 'you see that I am saving the best grapes for last? Is this not the thing to do in life?' The rabbi looked at him with a gentle smile. 'My son, eat the best first, and then with each bite, you will always be eating the best.' "

Mr. Reaf let the door slam shut.

* * *

There are moments in our lives when in the midst of performing a routine task, we suddenly see ourself through the eyes of another--as if one part of us stood back like a peeping Tom and watched ourself without the trappings of our own beliefs and prejudices. As Mr. Reaf stood peering through the cloud of frost billowing out of his open freezer, he realized what a creature of habit he had become. Inside were five distinct stacks of microwave dinners, each stack exactly five dinners high--his building blocks of nutrition that rarely altered from week to week. The far left stack was always Monday's meal: "Sirloin beef in a zesty barbeque sauce, green beans in lemony sauce, corn with red peppers, and apples in a plum sauce."

Next stack, each Tuesday's repast: "Grilled glazed turkey breast in a fruity sauce, green beans with smoky almonds in a seasoned sauce, corn bread with cranberries, and strawberry nonfat yogurt."

Every Wednesday: "Veal parmesan in a tangy tomato sauce, sliced peppers in a creamy cheese sauce, herb pasta and broccoli in a seasoned sauce, and raspberry crunch."

Thursday's menu: "Meat loaf meal in a tomato sauce, mashed potatoes topped in a buttery sauce, peas and carrots in a seasoned sauce, and chunky apple-raisin dessert."

Finally, Friday's banquet, his favorite: "Grilled chicken cordon bleu--a breast with rib meat on a slice of ham in a swiss cheese sauce with bacon bits, savory rice mixture in a buttery sauce, spinach gratin, corn with red peppers in a seasoned sauce, and a brownie."

Reaf reached up and pulled out Monday's beef. So this was what his life had come to, five stacks of too-bright vegetables, too-tasteless meats, and too-papery potatoes. What ever happened to home cooking? Since the divorce three years ago, he had just quit trying to fend for himself in the kitchen.

The thought of home-cooked meals reminded him of eating at his grandparents'. When he was little, the whole family used to go out to his grandpa's place in the country. As soon as you pulled open the squeaky screen door and stepped into the bright hallway of their house, your nose was filled with the most delicious smells. Biscuits rising on top of the stove, each soon to be a pocket for mounds of salty country ham; crispy fried chicken with lots of black pepper in the breading; sweet corn on the cob with real butter running in rivulets down its steaming sides; big bowls of mashed potatoes covered with thick brown chicken gravy; fresh Kentucky Wonder green beans just bursting with juice and ham seasoning; and always at least three desserts--homemade sweet potato pie with coconut and real whipped cream topping; peach cobbler with lots of cinnamon, brown sugar, and almond extract, topped with vanilla ice cream; and fig preserves to stuff inside that second pan of golden biscuits. After eating, his grandpa would sit in the corner in his old padded chair, calling Reaf over to tell him a story, to share some of his wisdom. Reaf always went reluctantly, thinking that whatever the old man had to say would be silly or stupid. Years later, however, he read a quote by Mark Twain that caused him to reconsider how he felt about grandpa's little talks. Twain said that when he was a boy of fourteen, his father was so ignorant he could hardly stand to have him around, but when he got to be twenty-one, he was astonished at how much his old man had learned in seven years.

His mind flashed to his grandpa in the hospital, still trying to smile as he called him over, hiding the pain from his cancer. Reaf was in college then, and grandpa asked him what he planned to do with his life.

"I'm not sure yet, grandpa," he said, fighting back the tears.

"Well, son, I'm gonna give you one more piece of advice. When you get out and find that job, watch yourself, no matter if you become a ditch digger or a brain surgeon. Because the ditch you're digging to survive can become a rut, and that rut can become your grave. Don't ever do what you hate, son. Life's too short."

His fingers suddenly ached with cold. "What the hell!" He tossed the beef back into the freezer and grabbed a chicken cordon bleu.

"This one's for you, grandpa."

Feeling giddy with his sudden rebellion, he opened the bottle of wine he usually saved for Friday and sat down with sixth period's letters. He could easily finish these and the dinner in time for *Monday Night Football.*

> Dear Landlord,
>
> Please read this letter. Cause you dont understand what you doing to me and my family. My sister she dont have a place to play. We got roaches and rats in our house. The hallway smells like pis and there aint no lite. We cant go out at night cause of drugs. A girl next door was killed a few months ago right in front of her ma. My mom says I must be the man of the house. I

dont want to. I want to play baseball. I just sixteen. Why dont you clean up our project. I hate where I live. We got trash and stinks everywhere. You not doing your job man.

Gracias Juan

Mr. Reaf never saw *Monday Night Football*, and he never saw sixth period the same way again.

Week Two, Day Two

As a man's desire is, so is his destiny. For as his desire is, so is his will; as his will is, so is his deed; and as his deed is, so is his reward, whether good or bad.

--The Upanishads

Mr. Reaf stood behind his desk watching first period push through the heavy metal door. Most of the kids automatically glanced up at the quote on the board as they entered. The quote had a strange effect on them. As their eyes found it, their bodies seemed to go into slow motion. They walked trance like, eyes never leaving the board, toward their seats. Then they would hover over their chairs as they finished reading, only to slide down into their seats with a somewhat dazed expression on their faces. Some would begin to talk, but most looked up at him expectantly.

"Good morning, first period. Today we are going to do something a bit different."

"Yes!" came a spontaneous burst from Tom in the back. A number of students chuckled.

"We normally discuss the quote for each day," Reaf continued, "but today, I'd like you to read it over, think about it for a while, perhaps jot down some ideas, then answer the following three questions, which I'll write on the board."

*What is your greatest desire, your dream in life?
*How do you expect to attain it?
*What rewards, good or bad, might you reap along the way?

"How long does it have to be, Mr. Reaf?" asked Rachel.

"You will write for the entire period. The length will vary for each student, depending on how much thought he or she puts into it."

"Are you going to grade it for grammar?" asked another student.

Reaf paused. "Well, no. At least not immediately."

"Do you want a five-paragraph theme?" asked another.

"No."

"Should each paragraph begin with a topic sentence?"

"If it seems appropriate."

The class grew quiet for a moment. Then Mary asked timidly, "What exactly do you want us to write?"

Reaf looked down at her, a bit irritated. "The answers to the questions on the board."

Nobody moved. Why all these questions, he thought. They usually just go straight to work. Wasn't this what they wanted, to do something different?

"Is there a problem?" he asked.

"Mr. Reaf?" said Rachel.

"Yes, Rachel."

"Well, what do I have to do to get an A?"

Reaf stared at Rachel, at all of them. They stared back, waiting for an answer. Of course, this was Honors. Their lives were grades. They played the school game better than anybody. But this morning he had changed the rules of the game, and they weren't sure how to respond. They could talk their hearts out, but putting something on paper implied a grade. Now they wanted to know exactly what hoops to jump through. He felt a devilish thrill run through him. Smiling, he said, "At this point there will be no grade, unless of course you don't do the assignment; then I will count it as a zero on a major test."

Instantly binders clicked open, the air rattled with the sound of paper being torn from spiral notebooks, muffled voices indicated the borrowing of pens, and then the noises subsided into an uneasy quiet as minds searched for answers.

* * *

The rest of the day went smoothly. Second and third periods dutifully set to work, but most ran out of steam within ten minutes. He found himself rushing from desk to desk, reading skeletons of essays. The kids were great on main ideas but had no idea how to add details to their writing. Like a waitress pouring coffee at a busy truck stop, Reaf hopped around the room, asking the same questions over and over:

*How would that make you feel?
*What else could happen?
*Why would you say that?
*Can you describe that more clearly?

He was beginning to feel a little successful at getting kids to write until fifth period walked in. They refused to do the assignment, but not in their usual, abusive manner. Instead, they just sat, quiet. Reaf asked if any students could give examples of a dream or goal. Silence. He threw out some examples of careers. Still nothing. In desperation, he decided to focus on one student. He'd take his chances with Ellis.

"Ms. Ellis, what's one of your goals?"

She stared at him blankly. No answer. The class grew uncomfortable. Students squirmed in their seats. Heads turned away when he looked them in the eye. He was losing his patience.

"Well, would you rather do grammar?" he said threateningly.

"Just pass out the worksheets, man," mumbled someone in the back of the room.

Mr. Reaf turned to see who had spoken. Ellis hunkered down in her seat.

"Ms. Ellis, surely you don't want to do grammar worksheets. Now, I've asked you once. *What* is one of your goals?"

All heads turned to Ellis. Reaf grew worried. He had challenged a classroom leader. A blatant refusal to cooperate now could lead to all-out rebellion.

"Mr. Reaf?" said Ellis cautiously, never lifting her eyes.

"Yes?"

She paused for a moment, then smiled and said, "I just want to get through this period."

Everyone burst out laughing, including Mr. Reaf. He had to give it to Ellis: she certainly had a knack for surprising him.

"Well, Ellis, I promise you that you'll achieve that goal. But what about after class. What then?"

She straightened up in her seat.

"Volleyball practice. I've got volleyball practice."

She had misunderstood his question. He almost stopped her to get her to focus on her future, but thought better of it.

"And what goal would you like to set?"

"I would like to set someone so we'd make a goal," she answered quickly. Her teammates around her laughed, and a number of high-five hand slaps were exchanged.

"Good, Ms. Ellis. Is there someone in particular you want to beat?"

All heads of the gang of five nodded in unison.

"Yeah, we play Valdez this week. They beat us last year in the regional. I want to beat them bad."

"Great, Ms. Ellis. How do you specifically plan to attain this goal?"

Ellis's eyes sparkled. "Well, coach says their weak point is the center. They don't cover well and get confused with assignments. She says we need to pound the ball again and again into the middle."

"How do you plan to do that, Ms. Ellis?"

"Well, we got to set out spikers at each end of the net . . ."

She went on and on, with Carter and Carlson and Macy jumping in every few seconds. Finally Reaf stopped her and asked her to write it all down.

"But I just told you everything!" she wailed.

"Yes, but in English class we are graded on what we write. So start writing, please."

Shaking her head, she pulled out an old, tattered notebook. No one else in the class moved. It had become clear to Reaf that many of these kids wouldn't or couldn't think in concrete terms about their distant futures. He wasn't sure why; maybe that was just too nebulous a concept for them. He found he needed to bring them closer to the present. So he asked them about goals they might have for the year. If they couldn't answer that, then he'd pull them back in time until they could set a specific goal, even if it were only something they wanted to do right after class.

Slowly, almost painfully, one by one, they settled into writing. By the bell, Reaf was exhausted from scurrying from seat to seat trying to keep them on task. He slumped down into his seat only to look up and see sixth period pour in.

"Hey, Mr. Reaf, I hear you make us write a big paper today," yelled Montoya as he fell into his seat. The boy leaned back, stretching his long legs into the aisle. His stance clearly said, "Just try and make me work."

"What's the matter, Mr. Reaf? You burn up the copy machine making worksheets?" called out Juan as he marched by his desk.

Well, they sure were testy today. He straightened up in his seat, then stood up as the room filled. A number of heads turned toward the board, struggling with the quotation.

"Sixth period, we will write today, but it will not be the same assignment as for the rest of the classes. I've read your letters, and today we're going to revise them. Tammy and Rhonda, please pass these out."

"Hey, I don't want them to see what I made!" yelled Montoya.

Reaf divided the stack of papers and handed them to two girls sitting in the front row. Dutifully, they began to pass out the papers.

"There are no grades on these papers. They will not be graded until you have rewritten them. On your papers you will see references to grammar errors you have made. Look those pages up in your grammar book and fix those mistakes first. If I had a question about content that you don't understand, then raise your hand and I'll come over and help you."

"What?" yelled out one student.

"Damn," yelled Montoya, "just put a grade on it."

He stared at the class. These were the kids who had yelled for these papers for days. Now he understood that it wasn't the letters they wanted. They just wanted to see a grade. That would mean they were through with it.

"Hey, Mr. Reaf," yelled Hernandez, "what's this quote mean?"

He glanced up at the board. "Well, Mr. Hernandez, let's use your letters as an example. Most of you, in fact I can safely say all of you, expressed a sincere desire to improve your living situation. To me the quote suggests that if this is truly your desire, then you must put your will behind it. In other words, some effort, some work, a deed. And only then can you find a reward. I think this is what the Upanishads are trying to tell us."

"So what do these Upanishits know? They're probably a bunch of fags, man," called out Montoya.

Mr. Reaf swung around to face Montoya. "Don't ever say that word!" he said between clenched teeth. "Don't ever use that term in here, you understand? I won't stand for that!"

The class sat in stunned silence, their eyes huge. Reaf was leaning over his desk, his fists balled up tight. They'd seen him mad, but they had never seen him straining so hard to hold in his anger. No one dared move. He took a deep breath and straightened up.

"Now let's get to work. No more comments or you're outta here."

Tammy and Rhonda finished passing out the papers. Someone snickered.

"Get to work!" he yelled. "No talking!"

The class settled down, but little work was done. Most just dawdled. When the bell rang, a number hurried to get outside, where he heard them burst into laughter.

Mr. Reaf sat behind his desk, staring down at his hands, one left finger extended. Sixth period was a definite loss, perhaps for the rest of the year. Now, the rumors would fly: Mr. Reaf is gay.

"Mr. Reaf?"

He looked up. Hernandez was standing in front of his desk.

"Hernandez?"

"Mr. Reaf, you not a . . . uh . . . uh?" Hernandez paused, searching for words.

"No, Hernandez. I'm not gay."

The boy's shoulders and face relaxed with his answer. "Man, then why you defending gays?"

Reaf sat silent for a moment, staring back down at his hands. Why should he tell this kid? What difference would it make? "Let's just say, Hernandez, that I knew one once."

"You knew a fa . . . uh, I mean a gay?" he asked incredulously.

"Hernandez, why are you asking me this?"

"I don't know, man. I'm just interested."

"Well, Hernandez, it's a long story that I won't bore you with right now."

"You not boring me. I want to hear it."

He looked back up at Hernandez. The boy seemed sincere about hearing him out.

"Hernandez, my older brother was gay."

"Was? Do you mean he got hisself straightened out?"

"Himself, Hernandez. And he did not 'get himself straightened out.' "

"Why's he gay, man?"

"I don't know why. Don't ask me," he said with exasperation. "My other brother and I are straight. I don't know what happened to David. But then, I don't understand why some people eat snails, and I don't understand why some people wear towels around their heads their entire lives. Nor do I understand why some people are born with certain talents and others can't seem to do anything. I don't understand a lot of things, Hernandez."

"You like your brother, Mr. Reaf?"

"Like him?" he shook his head. "Hernandez, he was my hero. He took care of me."

"Why you need taking care of, Mr. Reaf?" asked Hernandez.

Reaf looked down at his desk, a bit embarrassed. "Well, believe it or not, I was a pretty fat kid. I wasn't exactly a great athlete either."

"I can believe that, Mr. Reaf," Hernandez said, then laughed. "I just kidding with you Mr. Reaf. You skinny. You couldn't have been fat?"

"Well, I was. I lost the weight in college. But in junior high my classmates used to call me 'Beefy Reefy.' "

Hernandez laughed. "That's pretty funny, Mr. Reaf." Reaf gave him a look that squelched his laughter.

"Well, anyway," the teacher continued, "David, my brother, was always there for me. He made me get out and do things. I can still see him running alongside my bicycle the day we took the training wheels off, shouting words of encouragement. Or I can feel his arms around me at home plate, showing me when to swing the bat. He could do about anything. He loved to hunt. He lettered in basketball and baseball in high school, first string. He was handsome, and the girls went crazy for him. The phone rang all the time. Everybody loved him, and he'd do anything for anybody. You never heard him badmouthing anyone. He just wasn't that kind of person."

Reaf leaned forward and stared out the small, cloudy windows across the room. "When he went to Vietnam, I prayed everyday he'd make it through. Our whole family supported the war. He did, too. He thought he was doing the right thing for his country. And he made it, ya know. That's the great irony. Even comes back with a medal, a Purple Heart for some shrapnel from a land mine that his best buddy stepped on. But he's not the same. I mean, he's still nice, but he keeps talking about how precious life is, and how he's got to live it honestly. I can still see him sitting on the front stoop, just staring off into the distance. He grew quieter. I didn't know what to say to him anymore. Then one day he packed up and left."

"Where to?" asked Hernandez.

"He moved to New York City. After that we heard from him less and less. He began to come home only on holidays. I missed him a lot. I wanted to go spend a weekend with him, but he said it wasn't a good idea just then. The silence, the space between us grew and grew."

Mr. Reaf leaned back in his chair and looked down at his hands in his lap. "One day I got home after football practice and the phone was ringing. My folks were out Christmas shopping. Ya know, I can still hear that voice so clearly. I can remember exactly what the police officer said."

"Mr. Reaf? This is the New York City Police Department. I'm afraid we have some bad news for you about your son, David."

"Yes, sir," I said, thinking I should go get Dad, but my feet wouldn't respond. I just stood there holding the phone, listening.

"I'm afraid that your son has been murdered."

"What?" I yelled. "What are you saying? Why would anyone kill David?"

"Well," said the policeman, "it seems he and a friend were attacked in Greenwich Village by a gang of youths from New Jersey looking to beat up homosexuals."

"What?" I yelled. "Listen, mister, you've got the wrong family. My brother ain't no fag. You crazy or something, calling here with this kind of crap? You go to hell!" And I slammed the phone down.

Reaf looked back up at Hernandez. "But he didn't have the wrong family. They called back a few hours later when my folks were home. My dad had to drive up and identify the body. He had been stabbed twenty-three times. There were seven of them. He never had a chance."

Hernandez exclaimed something in Spanish. His eyes were wide with shock as he waited for his teacher to continue.

"We went up later that week to clean out his apartment. I guess that's when I began to realize David might really have been gay. There are so many of them in that neighborhood. Then I found a letter on his desk addressed to me."

"What kind of letter, Mr. Reaf?"

Reaf opened his briefcase. Reaching behind the flap on the top side, he dug down into one of the compartments and pulled out a thin, creased letter.

"I don't know when he was going to send me this. In it, he tries to explain about being gay, saying he always knew he was since he was a kid. He even copied the list of famous homosexuals from the *Book of Lists* to show me that a lot of well-known people were gay, too."

"Can I look at that, Mr. Reaf?" asked Hernandez.

He handed Carlos the letter. As Hernandez read, Reaf lowered his head on the desk. A cinder block had settled on his chest. Oh God, he thought, not here, not in front of Hernandez. He took a deep breath to try and ease the pain.

"Shoot, man, all these people were gay?" he asked in disbelief.

"Yeah, I guess so," Reaf said, looking back up at Hernandez, but his voice cracked.

Hernandez took a step back, startled.

"Yeah, well, look, Mr. Reaf, I got to get to practice. I'll see you tomorrow."

He turned and hurried out of the room. The teacher lowered his head back down on his desk. He pushed the tears back down. Slowly the pain turned to anger. Anger at having his guard down in front of Hernandez. Anger at the scum who killed his brother. God, would he love to catch those punks in a dark alley and blow their brains . . .

Suddenly the door groaned.

"Good afternoon, Mr. Reaf. I hope you had a pleasant day. Sorry I'm a little late, but . . ."

Reaf jerked his head up and shot Luis a look that stopped him dead in his tracks.

"Oh, excuse me, sir," he said, slightly bowing, his eyes wide and watching him. "Is there something you need me to do?"

He leaned back in his seat and took a deep breath. "Yeah, get me a gun to kill a bunch of creeps in New Jersey."

Luis tilted his head to the side, obviously confused. "In New Jersey, sir?" He shuffled a few feet toward his desk. "May I ask what anyone in New Jersey has done to wrong you?"

"Oh, nothing much," he said smugly. "They just killed my brother a few years ago."

Luis stopped short, his mouth open in surprise. "Oh, sir, I

am very sorry."

"Not as sorry as those kids will be if I ever get my hands on them," Reaf said and started stuffing papers into his briefcase.

"Mr. Reaf, your brother, he was killed a few years ago?"

"Yeah, that's right. Nineteen years."

"And you are still very hurt and angry about this?"

"Right again, Einstein," he said sarcastically and slammed the briefcase shut. "Wouldn't you be hurt if someone you loved died senselessly?"

"Yes, Mr. Reaf, I would be hurt." The janitor watched him as he got up and straightened the books on his desk. "Mr. Reaf, if you like, I might suggest a way to ease your pain for your brother."

Reaf looked at the janitor in disbelief. Does this guy ever know when to shut up? he wondered. "So tell me, Mr. Psychologist, how do I ease my pain?" Reaf asked dryly, picking up another stack of papers.

"Well, sir, it involves forgiveness."

The teacher's hand froze holding the stack of papers. He looked straight at Luis.

"How dare you?" he said angrily, then slammed the papers on the desk. Luis flinched. "How dare you ask me to forgive the scum that killed my brother. That is an anger I'll carry to my grave."

Luis paused, then said, "Sir, may I ask you something?"

"What?" Reaf yelled.

"What do you think your brother would wish for you today?" he asked in a soft voice.

His question caught Reaf off guard. He looked at Luis, puzzled. "What? How could I know that?"

"Well then," Luis said, "let me ask you this. If your brother hadn't been murdered, if he were still alive, what would you wish for him?"

Reaf looked down at his desk. Funny, he had fantasized speaking to his brother many times. There was so much he wanted to tell him.

"I guess, first, I'd just tell him I love him, no matter who he is."

"And why, sir, would you tell him this first?"

"Because I never got to tell him that before he died. And I would want him to be happy, to know that his little brother cared for him," Reaf said softly.

"Then, sir, perhaps even now, who can say, he wants the same for you. He just wants his little brother to be happy. But as long as you carry this anger inside, you will never be."

Reaf shoved the stack of papers into his briefcase. "Then that's the way it must be. That scum in New Jersey doesn't deserve forgiveness."

Luis leaned over the desk and looked Mr. Reaf squarely in the eyes. "But, sir, one doesn't forgive others for their benefit. We forgive others so that we may go on with our own lives. We forgive so that *we* may be happy."

Reaf pushed back in the chair, then closed the briefcase and snapped the locks shut. You couldn't talk to this idiot, he thought. He stepped around the desk and headed for the door. Pulling it open, Reaf offered a parting shot.

"Forget, hell. Some things are not worth letting go."

"Sir?"

The teacher paused inside the door opening. The cool September air blew past him into the stale room. "What?" he yelled.

"May I tell you a brief story?"

Reaf stood in the open doorway, staring outside, not knowing whether to listen or just slam the door and walk away. He looked back at the janitor and saw his eyes brighten.

"Mr. Reaf, many years ago two Buddhist monks went on a long pilgrimage. As part of their spiritual path, they had sworn an oath that they would live a life of celibacy--that they would never even touch a woman. One day they came to a swollen river. Beside the river was a woman who wanted to cross. One of the monks immediately picked her up and carried her through the raging current. For the next two days, the other monk fumed over the actions of his companion. Finally, in great anger he said, 'I don't understand you. You know we are sworn not to touch women. How could you have carried that woman across the river?'

"The other monk smiled gently at his friend and said, 'Yes, but I left her at the river bank. Why are you still carrying her now?' "

Luis's deep brown eyes sparkled. He smiled.

"Nonsense," Reaf said and slammed the door shut with a hollow thud.

Week Two, Day Three

One Half of you loves, and the Other Half of you at times hates. This is the Forked Medicine Pole of Man. The clever thing the Medicine has taught us here is this: One Half of you must understand the Other Half or you will tear yourself apart. It is the same with the Other Half of any People who live together. One must understand the Other, or they will destroy each other. But remember! Both Halves must try to understand.

--*Seven Arrows*
Hyemeyohsts Storm

Wednesday proved to be an especially easy day. The kids always loved this film about Chief Joseph. They were amazed at the wisdom and courage of the Nez Perce tribe as they outsmarted the U.S. Cavalry which chased them. Chief Joseph led some 750 men, women, and children on a 1,500-mile trek in the dead of winter across the Missouri River and the Rocky Mountains. Not unlike many Americans in those days, his students soon sided with the Indians and found themselves hoping that the tribe would make it safely across the Canadian border.

When General Miles finally caught Joseph and his ragtag tribe less than 40 miles from the border, the students became deathly quiet. The cavalry attacked the sick and exhausted Nez Perce for several days until the Indians finally gave up on October 5, 1877. More than one kid wiped an eye as Joseph gave his surrender speech:

> I am tired of fighting. Our chiefs are killed. Looking Glass is dead. Too-hool-hool-suit is dead. The old men are all dead. It is the young

> men who say no and yes. He who led the young men is dead. It is cold and we have no blankets. The little children are freezing to death. My people, some of them, have run away to the hills and have no blankets, no food. No one knows where they are--perhaps they are freezing to death. I want to have time to look for my children and see how many of them I can find. Maybe I shall find them among the dead. Hear me, my chiefs. I am tired. My heart is sad and sick. From where the sun now stands I will fight no more forever.

Many students throughout the day mentioned how well the day's quote fit the movie. Reaf made a note to himself to ask the Debate Club about the source of the quote and why they had chosen that one for today. The kids in second and third periods talked about how misunderstood the Indians had been. He told them how, when he was growing up, he was taught that Indians were dumb savages who slaughtered peaceful white settlers. No mention was made in the history books of the sophistication of the Native American culture before the advent of the white man.

Fifth and sixth periods saw an opportunity for a little white-bashing. In both classes, discussion reflected a belief that most of white America had never tried to understand any minority, but only accepted or tolerated them after being forced to by the government. Funny, but for the first time with these two classes, Reaf didn't feel that their comments were barbs aimed at him. Maybe they thought that since he was the one who showed them this film, then perhaps he was an Other Half they might try to understand.

As the door slammed shut behind the last student leaving sixth period, Reaf leaned back in his seat, plopped his feet on his desk, and closed his eyes. A grin spread slowly across his face. He didn't even need to do the finger count. He knew he had experienced one of those very rare days. He had batted a thousand. Every period was a win. Why couldn't more days be like this? The door hinges groaned loudly.

"Come in," he said with his eyes still closed. "I'll be out of your way in a moment."

"Excuse me, Mr. Reaf."

Reaf jumped in his seat. Hernandez! What was he doing here?

Self-consciously he removed his feet from the top of the desk and brushed the yellow chalk dust off his pants cuffs. "I thought you were the janitor," he said quickly.

"No, sir, but I just saw Luis. He said to tell you he has been called to the principal's office. He will clean your room later."

"Oh, well, thanks, Hernandez, but you didn't really have to come back to tell me that."

"I didn't come to tell you that," he replied, walking slowly toward the teacher's desk. Reaf straightened up in his seat, reached over, and hit the rewind button on the video.

"I came to apologize for having to leave yesterday when you were telling me about your brother. The coach, he would have killed me if I had been late for practice," he said softly, eyes lowered. The tall boy stood in front of Reaf's desk, hands in his pockets.

Embarrassed, Reaf began stuffing papers into his briefcase.

"That's okay, Hernandez. Let's just forget about it, okay?" he said without looking up at him.

Hernandez remained silent, watching him. Mr. Reaf looked over at the video machine. God, it was taking forever for this film to rewind.

"Is that all, Hernandez?" he finally asked.

"No. I wanted to say something else."

Surprised, Reaf looked up at him. The boy swallowed hard and shifted his books from one arm to another.

"What, Hernandez?"

"Well, I think I know how you feel."

"What do you mean, Hernandez?" he asked. "Know what I feel about what?"

"Well, Mr. Reaf, two summers ago I lost someone, too. My sister. She was twelve. Where I stay at, we live on the first floor. I told my mom when we moved in that we shouldn't stay on the first floor. But she wanted to stay there 'cause my *abuela*, my grandmother, can't walk good. Anyway, my sister was leaning out the window talking to her friend. The next thing she's laying on the living room floor with half her head missing. She landed on top of my little brother. My mom, she just screamed and grabbed them both in her arms. My sister's brains poured out everywhere."

"Oh God," Reaf whispered. Hernandez continued, almost mechanically.

"I was at practice, so I didn't see it happen. One of the neighbors ran and got me. When I got home my mom was still sitting in the middle of the floor holding her. I couldn't believe it, Mr. Reaf. Some asshole just rode by in a car and blew my little sister away."

Reaf was dumbstruck. Covering his mouth with his hand, he stared at this high school boy. How could this child survive the scene he was describing and not be affected deeply? How could he not be driven crazy living with such horror? Hernandez leaned over the teacher's desk. His eyes flashed with anger. His voice was tight with emotion now.

"Mr. Reaf, I get so angry, man. I go out that night and try to find out who did this. I'm going to kill them. I borrow a piece from a friend. But it was some gang in some other part of town. We never find out who did it. And nobody would say they saw anything."

He paused for a moment. His chest heaved slightly, and Reaf saw him swallow hard. The boy straightened up and wiped his right eye with his shirt sleeve.

"You know the worst part, Mr. Reaf? You may think this is dumb, but the landlord, he made me the maddest of all. He told my mom that he would not change the carpet with the blood stains in it. 'It was too new,' he said. We couldn't stand looking at it, so I went to a thrift store and bought a little rug to cover the stain. But we all know it's there. Nobody ever steps on it."

Reaf shook his head in disbelief. "Herna . . . uh, Carlos, couldn't your gang have found out who did it and told the police?"

"I don't belong to no gang, Mr. Reaf," Hernandez said softly, staring down at the floor.

"What? You're not in a gang?" the teacher asked incredulously.

"No, sir. They wanted me. And I wanted their help to kill those guys. But my mom, she beg me not to. So did my *abuela*. They didn't want any more bloodshed. This year at school, though, they came after me again. I almost joined, too. Then I talked to Luis one day, and he kind of set me straight."

"Luis? You mean that Mexican janitor?"

Hernandez grinned. "He's not Mexican, Mr. Reaf."

Reaf looked down at his desk. "Oh, excuse me, Hernandez. I just thought . . . well, I mean, I figured that since you two knew each other maybe you had the same background." He raised his eyes to Hernandez. The boy smiled.

"That's okay, Mr. Reaf. Actually, I think he's Salvadoran. But he's pretty cool."

Mr. Reaf looked at Hernandez with curiosity. It seemed odd that this big kid, this star on the football team, was taking advice from the school janitor. The same guy who worried him silly at the end of each day.

"Well, what did Luis say about gangs?"

Hernandez laughed. "What didn't he say. Man, that guy can talk for hours."

"I know!" the teacher was laughing.

"Well, first he quoted some Chinese priest about doing people good. So I asked him, 'Even if they've been bad to you? Does that mean I'm suppose to let these bangers come into my house?'

" 'No,' he says. Then he quotes some holy dude from the Arab land somewhere. He called the guy a sufi wordish."

"That's *dervish*. They were priests in Afghanistan and Turkey, I think."

"Yeah, that's it. Dervish. Anyway, I couldn't remember everything he said, so I asked him to write it down. I carry it in my wallet."

"Would you mind if I saw what he wrote?"

"No problem."

Hernandez reached in his back pocket and pulled out a long wallet. A chain connected one corner of the wallet to his belt loop. Pulling apart the velcro, he rummaged in one side, then the other until he found a scrap of notebook paper. On it, written in a beautiful script, were the following words.

> Those who are good I treat as good. Those who are not good I also treat as good. In so doing I gain in goodness.
>
> --Lao Tzu
> from the *Tao Te Ching*

"Humph," Reaf said. "And where's his advice about not getting involved with gang members?"

"Turn it over," he said, pointing to the paper.

Reaf flipped it over.

> Make no friendship with an elephant-keeper
> If you have no room to entertain an elephant.
>
> --Saadi of Shiraz
> Sufi Master

Reaf burst out laughing. He looked up at Hernandez, who was smiling broadly.

"That is pretty funny, ain't it?" the boy said. "But you know, it makes a lot of sense. I don't want those guys in my house."

Still chuckling, Reaf reread the quote.

"You're right. It does make good sense."

He reached up to hand the paper back to Hernandez, when suddenly something about it caught his eye. Why did it look so familiar?

"Carlos, did you write this down?"

"No, Luis wrote it."

He looked up at the board, at today's quote, at the identical meticulous lettering inscribed there. He couldn't believe his eyes. Oh God, this little man, this janitor, not the Debate Club, had been leaving those quotes on his board. But why? Why would he?

"Mr. Reaf?" Hernandez asked uncertainly, reaching for the slip of paper. Reaf was still holding his arm outstretched toward the board. Carlos took the scrap of paper and replaced it in his wallet.

"I got to go. I'll be late for practice."

Mr. Reaf sat staring at the board, at today's quote. No wonder it fit the film so well. Hernandez started to move away.

"Oh, yeah . . . listen, Carlos. Thank you for sharing that with me. I mean, I think you're doing the right thing."

As the boy pulled the heavy door toward him, he turned and smiled.

"Sure, Mr. Reaf. No problem."

Week Two, Day Four

Many men go fishing all of their lives without knowing that it is not fish they are after.

--Henry David Thoreau

Mr. Reaf had not been able to get the janitor off his mind all evening. On one hand, he was angry that the man had slipped those quotes in under his nose without ever acknowledging that he had written them. What the hell was his agenda? he wondered. Who the hell did he think he was, a teacher?

Yet, on the other hand, Reaf had to admit that the quotes had turned out to be a positive feature. The kids had established a pattern of talking about them at the beginning of each period. Starting each class off the same way every day had caused his discipline problems, at least at the beginning of the period, to decrease. But why was this man doing this? And where the hell did he get these sayings?

As Reaf entered first period on Thursday, he immediately glanced at the board. Sure enough, another new quote was inscribed there. Various students in first period were already intent on sharing what they thought the quote meant. He purposely set his briefcase on the desk at a slight angle so that it fell over with a resounding smack. A cloud of chalk dust billowed up at him. As he fanned away the dust, first period settled down.

"Mr. Reaf?"

"Yes, Tom."

"Today's quote doesn't make any sense. How can somebody go fishing and not know he's fishing, unless he's on drugs or something?"

A number of students chuckled. All heads turned to Reaf for an answer. One thing he had learned in teaching was how to dodge a bullet.

"Would anyone like to answer Tom's question?"

"Mr. Reaf?"

"Yes, Joanna?"

"I'm not sure I can answer it. But I do know a story my granddaddy from North Carolina tells about fishing."

Groans erupted like bubbles rising in a pot of hot soup.

"Joanna," called out Paul. "This is about fish, not veal. You got your meals mixed up, girl!" A number of students laughed.

"Class, quiet down. Joanna, does this have anything to do with the quote?"

"I think so, sir," she responded meekly.

"Well, go ahead, then."

Joanna sat up in her seat. Her eyes brightened as she began to tell her story.

"Well, ya see. There's this guy sitting by the pond fishing. Well, he's actually just keeping his line wet and drowning worms, as my granddaddy says, 'cause he's not catching that many fish. All of a sudden, this Yankee businessman comes tearing through the bushes making all kinds of noise."

"What?" yelled Rachel. "Ah, come on, a Yankee? Easy on the local color, Joanna."

Joanna looked at Reaf for support.

"Go ahead, Joanna. I guess a little regional flavor makes the story more interesting."

"Okay," Joanna said excitedly. She obviously liked telling this story. "So, this Yankee says to the guy fishing, 'Buddy, you need to get a little more serious about this fishing here. Do you realize what an opportunity you're missing?'

"The fisherman shakes his head no. He never takes his eyes off the bobber.

"The businessman says, 'Look, buddy, if you were to put three or four lines in the water, you could pull in a lot more fish.'

" 'Yep,' says the fisherman, still staring at the bobber.

" 'And with all those fish, you could open up a little

roadside stand out there on the highway. As you sold more and more fish, you could pay people to come in and do your fishing for you. And with those profits you could get a boat and a net and just scoop gobs of fish right out of this pond. Why, pretty soon you'd have big rigs pulling in here all day, shipping your fish all over the country. You'd be worth millions!'

"The businessman looked at the fisherman for some sign of enthusiasm, but the fisherman just sat there staring at the bobber," continued Joanna.

" 'Aren't you even interested?' asks the businessman, who was losing his patience with the fisherman.

" 'Nope.'

" 'Why not?' yells the businessman.

" 'What would I do with all that money?' replies the fisherman.

" 'What would you do with all that money? You could take time off from your busy schedule. My God, man, with lots of money you could do anything you want. Think about it, what would you do?'

"The fisherman looked at the Yankee and said, 'I'd go fishing.' "

Caught by surprise, everyone in the room burst into laughter. The girl behind Joanna patted her on the back. She leaned back in her seat as if she had just played a winning ace.

"Good story, Joanna," Mr. Reaf said, still chuckling, "but can anyone explain what it says about today's quote?"

Tom raised his hand.

"Tom?"

"Well, I guess maybe it means that sometimes what we're doing may have more than one purpose. I mean, this guy didn't seem to care how many fish he caught. He was more interested in just taking it easy in life."

Rachel raised her hand.

"Rachel?"

"I think the quote really applies to the businessman. He's so focused on making money that it's the only way he can see the world. He doesn't even understand why the guy is fishing."

She paused and lowered her eyes to her desk. "He sort of reminds me of my dad. He never slows down."

A few students shifted nervously in their seats.

"Well, are we ever guilty of acting this way?" Reaf asked the class.

"I think some boys are like the businessman. They miss the point when they're trying to get a girl in bed," called out Joanna.

"Here we go again," said Tom.

"Well, it's true," she continued. "They're so interested in getting laid, they don't understand that to some people having sex might be a part of something much bigger."

The direction of the discussion was getting a little too risqué for Reaf. "Who else can think of another example of this quote?"

A number of hands shot up.

"Okay, then let's write about it, since each of you seems to have his own ideas. Explain what the quote means to you."

"Can we use examples from history?" called out Randy, a bespectacled student who sat in the corner and rarely said anything.

"Uh, sure. Why not? Any example you can come up with, as long as it supports the quote. While you're working on that, I'll pass back the papers you wrote describing your life's dream. I want you to rewrite these, fixing the grammatical errors I've marked. If you don't know how to fix them, look 'em up in your grammar book. But don't bother me."

The students settled down to work. As they began to jot down ideas, Reaf passed out their papers. Few students focused on the new assignment, however, until they had seen what they had made on the papers being returned. Smiling, he watched them furtively scan the papers for a grade.

"Mr. Reaf?" called out Rachel.

"Yes."

"You forgot to grade mine."

"No, Rachel. I have not put a grade on your papers at this point."

"But you didn't even make any comments about what I said.

You just marked grammatical errors."

Her voice had the same ring of disappointment as that of a spoiled child who realizes that a parent has returned from a trip without gifts. Obviously the entire room felt the same, since they were all scowling at their teacher. Their papers had been very insightful. Reaf hadn't thought much about what some of these kids wanted to be. He figured they'd just follow in their parents' footsteps, since most of them had plenty of money. He assumed they'd all go to college and, unless they got caught up in drugs or alcohol, probably be successful. But he had to admit that a few of them surprised him. Sure, Tom wanted to be a doctor just like his dad. Paul a lawyer. But Joanna wanted to be a congresswoman, and Rachel wanted to be a teacher.

"To be honest, Rachel," he explained, "I didn't know how to comment on what you wrote. I mean, what was I supposed to say regarding content? 'No, you can't be what you said you want to be'?"

A few kids chuckled as they began to see his point.

"So I tried to comment on how well you expressed your ideas. Okay?"

Rachel smiled. Who knew, maybe she was just trying to understand how she might handle a similar assignment with her students someday.

* * *

The rest of the day went pretty smoothly. A boy in third period told a story about how his dad had finally taken him fishing after years of promising to find the time to do it. His father was a high-strung investment analyst. Once on the pier, his father had been unable to stand in one place for more than a few minutes. He was constantly pulling in his line, moving down the pier between other fishermen, and stabbing another squirming worm, until each poor creature looked like a mess of pulp dangling from the hook. With almost every cast, he threw his line over someone else's. Apologizing profusely, his father would try to direct the other fishermen on the pier in order to separate the lines. More than once a fisherman took the rod from his father's hand in order to straighten out the mess. As the boy talked, students squirmed in their seats and looked down at their desks, embarrassed.

They didn't catch a single fish all day. Finally, in disgust, the father shoved the carton of live worms in a trash bin at the end of the pier. They drove home in silence until his father pulled into a fast-food restaurant. When the lady behind the counter offered the fish sandwich special the two looked at each other, smiled, then ordered burgers and fries. The fishing trip became one of those taboo topics that families silently agree not to bring up again.

Sixth period, of course, took the discussion to a whole other level. Johnson started it off by saying the quote described what the white man did to the Indians.

"What you talking 'bout, girl?" yelled Tanya Richards, one of her buddies.

"Yes, Ms. Johnson, please explain," Reaf added.

"Well, you know," she started, "them white soldiers were after one kind of fish, and it wasn't the kind of fish they thought they were after."

"Girl, you better go home and lay down, 'cause you ain't making no sense," called out Richards. Most of the students laughed loudly.

"Ms. Johnson, I don't think you've made yourself very clear."

"Well, give me a second!" she yelled. She straightened up in her seat. "I'll explain it if you tell these fools to be quiet."

"Quiet down, please," Reaf called out sternly. The class settled down.

"You see, the white folks thought the Indians were savages. That's what they had been taught to believe. That's the kind of fish they were after. But the Indians weren't savages at all. They had their stuff together. They were much smarter than the white man. In fact, they weren't even playing in the same pond as those sorry white soldiers. So, you see, it's like the man said, the white soldiers were fishing for one kind of person and didn't even realize it wasn't that kind of fish they were after. That's why they couldn't catch them."

Sanford in the back yelled out, "Tell it, girl!" Richards leaned over and gave her a high-five hand slap. The girl behind Johnson patted her on the back. Reaf shook his head in surprise.

"Shoot, man, they still be doing the same thing." All heads in the room turned to the back corner, to Sanford, who was slouched in his chair, just back from a few days' suspension. Mr. Reaf didn't know whether to encourage or ignore him. Perhaps he had learned his lesson.

"What exactly do you mean, Mr. Sanford?" Reaf asked in a tone that warned of immediate expulsion if he started something.

"Well shi--shoot, man. White folks still be treating others the same way they treated the Indians."

"Aren't you generalizing a bit, Mr. Sanford?" Reaf asked.

"Well, they be generalizing on me. Shoot, every time you go in a store they be watching you, following you, standing right in your face with their arms folded. They be expecting you to steal something."

"I hear that!" yelled out Jeffrey, another black student. A number of students began to describe similar occurrences. Reaf walked around his desk and stood in front of it.

"So, what you're saying, Mr. Sanford, is that these owners see thieves where there are none."

Sanford sat up straight in his seat. "Man, they assume 'cause you black you gonna steal something."

Without thinking, Reaf asked, "Well, do you?" He immediately took half a step back. Oh God, he thought. He's going to shoot me right here in my classroom!

Sanford never flinched. "I tell you what's the truth. Sometimes I do, just to show 'em I can beat them at their own game."

In the back of Reaf's mind, an education professor's voice called out, "Self-fulfilling prophecy."

"Is there any way you could change the situation, Mr. Sanford?"

Sanford grinned. He knew he had the stage, and he liked it.

"Let's just say that if any of those white fishermen go fishing for me, they gonna find out this shark has one hell of a bite."

Shouts of approval went up in the air from a number of students. Okay, Reaf thought, time to get off this subject. Those damn quotes.

"Yes, well . . . let's move on." He reached for the grammar book.

"Why people like that, Mr. Reaf?" blurted out Richards. "Why they label you something you not?"

The teacher looked up at her. To his surprise the entire class was looking at him. But on their faces registered real curiosity instead of the usual anger or indifference. They really wanted an answer, and they seemed to believe, or hope, he had one.

"Ms. Richards, I can't say that I know for sure. I guess we believe what we're taught to believe."

"Yeah, like if you live in the 'hood, then you must be a banger, huh, Mr. Reaf?"

Stung, Reaf looked over at Hernandez, who was grinning slyly.

"Yes, Hernandez. I think your point is well taken."

"Mr. Reaf," called out Jose. "*Mi madre*, she told me a story about such people."

"Is it a story you can repeat in school, Jose?"

Jose jabbed a finger at Reaf. "Forget you, man, if you don't want to hear what my mama said, then . . ."

"No, no, I'm sorry. Go ahead and tell your story. Just watch your language."

"Okay," he said, smiling. "Well, you see, there were these two gringo border guards working down in Texas. These cops thought they were real sharp. They figured they could catch any Mexican who tried to smuggle something across the border. Well, one day this old guy leads a donkey just packed full of stuff up to their gate. It was right near the end of their shift. One of the guards says to the other, 'Man, this old man is smuggling something for sure. Let's shake him down.' So the guards pull the Mexican over and spend about two hours going through his stuff."

"Hey, I thought you said it was near the end of their shift. You got these guys working overtime," yelled Sanford from the back.

"Let him tell the story, man," Hernandez shouted back. The two exchanged angry looks.

"So," continued Jose, "they couldn't find anything on him. Well, later in the week, the old man comes through again, and the two guards are still sure he's got something on him. So they pull him over again, search through everything, but can't find nothing.

"Well, this goes on for months until finally the guards give up. Then, years later, after one of the guards has retired, he's down in Mexico with his wife. He looks over and he sees the old man with the donkey. The guard says to the man, 'Hey, fella. Didn't you used to go across the border with a loaded donkey?'

"The old man says, 'Si.'

" 'Well, look,' says the gringo. 'I used to be a border guard. I don't work anymore, so I can't bust you. I just want to ask you something: Were you smuggling anything?'

" 'Si,' says the Mexican.

" 'I knew it,' says the gringo. 'I knew you were bringing in something. What was it?'

Jose paused and grinned, much the way the Mexican must have. 'Donkeys!' he yelled. 'Hah! Got you!' "

Taken completely by surprise, the room burst into laughter. Reaf stood in front of his desk with a wide grin. Jose leaned back, laughing at his classmates. Juan and Hernandez reached over and slapped him on the head.

Jose's story was like rain on a field. Stories popped up like weeds all over the classroom. Reaf decided to let the students talk the rest of the period, though he wasn't sure whether they were still discussing Thoreau's quote or not. He wasn't even sure where the discussion was going half the time. But he was sure of one thing: every kid in this room was listening, and Reaf hadn't yelled at a single person yet. Thirty minutes later, when the bell rang, they were still trading fish stories.

* * *

After sixth period filed out, Mr. Reaf leaned back in his chair, propped his feet up on his desk, and stared down at his hands. They looked cleaner than usual. Not nearly so much chalk dust on them. Made sense, he thought. He hadn't written any grammar sentences on the board for a few days. Then it dawned on him. He also hadn't kept score for a few days. How strange, he thought. He'd been scoring his classes at the end of the day for years. How could he have stopped doing something he'd always done and hardly notice?

Reaf looked up at the door, anticipating its groan as the little man leaned his weight against it. Where was he? He pulled his feet off the desk and stood up. What was he going to say to him? He looked up at the quote on the board. Where did he get this stuff? Picking up a pencil, he began drumming it on top of his briefcase. Hurry up, Luis, he thought. I've got a faculty meeting in fifteen minutes, and I've got a bone to pick with you!

He realized he had better go ahead and pack up. As he turned around to gather some papers for the faculty meeting, he heard the door groan loudly.

"Well, it's about time," Reaf said without turning around. "Running a little late today? Out looking for some words of wisdom, perhaps?" he added sarcastically, with his back still toward the door.

"Mr. Reaf, we always get here about now," said a young voice.

Reaf whirled around. There stood the members of the Debate Club, huddled half inside the door, half out.

"Oh, yes. Well . . . I guess you do. Hey, you haven't seen that janitor, have you?"

"You mean me, sir?" came a voice from outside. A broom attached to an arm slipped through the students, followed by the rest of the little man.

"Yes, uh, listen, kids, I'd like to have a word with this gentleman in private. I've got a faculty meeting in ten minutes. How about you come back then?"

"Sure, Mr. Reaf," the kid in front answered. Reaf smiled. Some kids will do almost anything with no questions asked, while others will make you wish you'd never asked at all. Luis leaned his broom against the wall and shuffled over to Reaf's desk. He looked at the teacher intently, his big brown eyes sparkling. Reaf looked down at his desk.

"Yes, well, look, uh . . . Mr. uh . . ." Reaf realized he wasn't even sure of his real name. "You know, we've never really been introduced."

"Mr. Argueta," Luis said, grinning and extending his hand.

"Argueta?" Reaf asked, taking his hand. "How do you say that again?"

The janitor shook his hand vigorously. "Argueta," he replied.

"Argueta," Reaf repeated, then pulled his hand away. "Mr. Argueta. I want to ask you something."

"Yes?"

Reaf looked down at his desk, then back at him. "Mr. Argueta, why have you been leaving these quotes on my board each day?"

"Oh, have you enjoyed them?"

"Well, yes, I guess you could put it that way. But, Mr. Argueta, why have you been doing this?"

A look of concern came over the janitor's face. "Mr. Reaf, I hope I did not offend you or cause you any problems."

"No, no. I'm just curious why you did it."

"Well, sir, from the first day I entered your classroom, I sensed a lot of anger in here. In fact, your students made a number of angry remarks about the class as they walked across the campus."

"What were they saying?" Reaf blurted out. Luis took a half step back.

"Well, Mr. Reaf, I do not pretend to speak for your students. Let us just say that in general they seemed very unhappy with what was taking place in your room."

"Well, school isn't for fun and games, Argueta," Reaf said defensively.

"Yes, sir, but you also seemed unhappy, sitting there behind your desk, staring down at your hands. I felt that perhaps I might offer something positive in your room."

"So, you were trying to change things, huh?" Reaf said accusingly.

Luis smiled. "Mr. Reaf. I do not have to try to change things. Things change, whether we attend to them or not. But there is no surer sign of a need for change than pain or unhappiness. I was simply trying to direct change down a more positive path by offering you a few more choices."

"And you thought the quotes would do this?" Reaf asked a bit angrily.

"The quotes were merely seeds. I had no idea whether you or anyone would cultivate them."

"Well, Mr. Argueta, I appreciate your good intentions, but I have no intention of changing the way I teach, for you or anybody else. I've managed to survive for a number of years just as I am."

Luis's eyes grew wide. He stepped toward Reaf's desk.

"I'm afraid, Mr. Reaf, that it may be too late to take such a stand."

"What do you mean?" the teacher asked loudly.

"I mean that things have already changed in your room."

"How would you know what I do in here?" Reaf asked loudly, leaning over his desk. "What are you talking about? What do you know about teaching methods? Just because I find some research on grammar, you think I'm going to go through some kind of metamorphosis. Well, forget your Kafka, Argueta."

The little man shuffled from one foot to the other, chuckling.

"That was very good! Kafka, metamorphosis. Very good!" he said, smiling broadly. "But it would seem your students think differently."

Reaf straightened up. "What? What are you talking about?"

"Well, sir, your sixth-period students now leave your room no longer angry. They leave excited about what's happening in here. They are beginning to speak very respectfully of you."

"What?" He sank slowly into his seat. Luis edged closer.

"Yes, Mr. Reaf. I'm afraid your students are beginning to like not only your class but you also."

Reaf looked away, up at the board. " 'Many men go fishing all of their lives without knowing that it is not fish they are after.' Argueta?"

"Sir?"

"Look, don't get your hopes up. The past few days, well, it's all a façade. I can't keep this up. I only know how to teach grammar. I can't keep going on day after day faking it with these quotes. I don't know what I'm doing in here. I need to get back to my lesson plans, to my same old structure, to--"

"Excuse me if I interrupt you, Mr. Reaf, but I think you do know what you are doing. It's just that instead of following your old system, you have begun to follow your own instincts, your intuition--perhaps as you once did."

"But, Argueta, you've got to have material to teach. You've got to have a plan, a scope and sequence of objectives. Teaching is not shooting from the hip everyday about philosophical ideas."

"I would agree, sir. Order is still called for. If you are interested, there are a few things I might suggest using."

Suddenly Reaf remembered the faculty meeting and looked down at his watch. "Shit!"

"That's not quite what I had in mind, sir."

"No, no, excuse me," said Reaf, laughing. "But I've got a faculty meeting that's starting right now."

He grabbed his briefcase and headed around the desk. Luis slowly turned, watching him. As he pulled on the heavy metal door, he stopped and looked back at the janitor.

"Argueta, perhaps we can talk about this some more?"

"I think tomorrow will be the best day, Mr. Reaf," he answered.

"Okay, but don't get any grand illusions about me changing my methods, hear? I'm not here to save the world, I just want to get through, and that means being me."

Luis tilted his head to the side, thinking. "Interesting, Mr. Reaf. You and Elie Wiesel tell the same story."

"Elie Wiesel, the Nobel Prize winner? What do you mean?" he asked, standing inside the open door.

"Well, sir, Mr. Wiesel tells of a rabbi who said that when you die, the creator will not ask you why you didn't become a great saviour, or leader, or prophet that answered life's mysteries. No, the creator will simply ask why you didn't become you, why you didn't use the gifts with which you were born to become the fully realized miracle you had the potential of becoming."

Reaf stared at the little man standing by his desk, wearing the same white shirt, brown vest, and black pants. Where does he get this stuff? He shook his head and let the door slam shut.

Week Two, Day Five

A tree that can fill the space of a man's arms
Grows from a downy tip;
A terrace nine stories high
Rises from small loads of earth;
A journey of a thousand miles
Starts from beneath one's feet.

--*Tao Te Ching*
Lao Tzu

The rusty hinges on the quonset hut door groaned as Mr. Reaf leaned against it. Funny how sounds, tastes, or smells will spark related images in your mind. He never smelled roofing tar without thinking of his childhood in Jacksonville, Florida, and the housing construction that was taking place everywhere around his own house, and he never heard "The Nutcracker" without remembering his ignominious part in the elementary school production of the ballet--as King Rat.

As he headed for his desk, the groaning hinges of the door suddenly reminded him of an old summer job he had had on the railroad. Standing on a siding, he would watch the old boxcars come rolling in, swaying on the rickety track and moaning under the loads they bore. He laughed to himself, realizing that the students who had entered through his quonset hut door for years sounded much the same, always moaning about the loads they bore.

Out of habit, he glanced up at the board to read the day's quote as he set his briefcase on the desk. Boy, ol' Argueta never lets up. Most of the kids had already read it. Some were offering their interpretations to each other.

His briefcase slid to one side as he let go of the handle, and he realized he had set it on top of something. Lifting it up, Mr. Reaf found an old book underneath. A yellow Post-it was stuck to its cover. The writing was unmistakable.

> Dear Mr. Reaf,
>
> Before we talk this afternoon, I thought that perhaps you might wish to try a small experiment. I have provided a book of short stories for you with one marked in particular. Your students might find it interesting.
>
> Sincerely,
> Luis Argueta

Reaf opened the book to a page that had been dog-eared. The story was titled "A Blind Man Catches a Bird."

What's he expect me to do with only one copy, he thought. I don't have the time or the paper to run to the lounge and make copies for the class. Shaking his head, he laid the book down and reached for his lesson-plan book to see where the class should be in the grammar text. It was time to get back on track.

"Mr. Reaf?"

"Yes, Brandon."

"What's a terrace?"

Reaf realized Brandon was talking about the quote on the board. "Anyone want to help Brandon out and tell him what a terrace is?" he asked, thumbing through the lesson-plan book.

"Isn't it how people in Asia grow crops, Mr. Reaf?" called out Rachel. "They carve the land on hillsides to look like steps."

"Yes, I think that's right, Rachel."

"Mr. Reaf?"

"Yes, Rachel," he said, looking up.

"Why did you choose this quote today?"

His stomach went into a small knot. "Well, Rachel . . . I . . . I . . ."

The class quieted down and looked at him expectantly.

"To be honest, Rachel, I didn't write the quote up there."

He paused and looked down at his desk. "In fact, I haven't put any of the quotes on the board."

Reaf raised his eyes to a room of confused faces.

"Mr. Reaf!" exclaimed Tom suddenly in a mock parental tone. "Have you been taking credit for someone else's writing?" He shook his finger at the teacher as he spoke.

Reaf smiled and felt his shoulders sag a bit. "Let's just say, Tom, I've been taking advantage of someone else's reading."

"Who's been putting the quotes up there, then?" asked Paul earnestly.

For some reason he didn't want to tell them it was Luis.

"Oh, some rascal who likes to incite change."

"Well, whoever it is," said Paul, "he's got my vote. Anything's better than that tired, old grammar book."

Reaf set the lesson-plan book down.

"So, Mr. Reaf, what journey are we starting today?" asked Tom with a sly grin on his face.

He looked down at the old volume of short stories, then back up at the class. "How 'bout I read you a story?"

Half the mouths in the room dropped open, like those of baby birds greeting a hungry mother. Reaf laughed out loud.

"Oh, come on. Don't be so shocked. I can read. We have a short period, anyway, because of the assembly. So, put your books under your desks, sit back, and just listen." He paused; no one moved. "If you don't, I'll test you on the story when I'm finished."

Immediately, books hit the floor, heads were lowered on desks, and long legs stretched into the aisles.

"Mr. Reaf?"

"Yes, Brandon."

"Can we turn the lights out?"

"Only if you wish me to go blind, Brandon."

"A Blind Man Catches a Bird"
A Zimbabwean Folk Tale
retold by Alexander McCall Smith

A young man married a woman whose brother was blind. The young man was eager to get to know his new brother-in-law, and so he asked him if he would like to go hunting with him.

"I cannot see," the blind man said. "But you can help me see when we are out hunting together. We can go."

The young man led the blind man off into the bush. At first they followed a path that he knew, and it was easy for the blind man to tag along behind the other. After a while, though, they went off into thicker bush, where the trees grew closely together and there were many places for the animals to hide. The blind man now held onto the arm of his sighted brother-in-law and told him many things about the sounds that they heard around them. Because he had no sight, he had a great ability to interpret the noises made by animals in the bush.

"There are warthogs around," he would say. "I can hear their noises over there."

Or "That bird is preparing to fly. Listen to the sound of its wings unfolding."

To the brother-in-law, these sounds were meaningless, and he was most impressed at the blind man's ability to understand the bush although it must have been for him one great darkness.

They walked on for several hours, until they reached a place where they could set their traps. The blind man followed the other's advice and put his trap in a place where birds might come for water. The other man put his trap a short distance away, taking care to disguise it so that no bird would know that it was there. He did not bother to disguise the blind man's trap, as it was hot and he was eager to get home to his new wife. The blind man thought that he had disguised his trap, but he did not see that he had failed to do so and any bird could tell that there was a trap there.

They returned to their hunting place the next day. The blind man was excited at the prospect of having caught something, and the young man had to tell him to keep quiet, or he would scare all the animals away. Even before they reached the traps, the blind man was able to tell that they had caught something.

"I can hear birds," he said. "There are birds in the traps."

When he reached his trap, the young man saw that he had caught a small bird. He took it out of the trap and put it in a pouch that he had brought with him. Then the two of them walked toward the blind man's trap.

"There's a bird in it," he said to the blind man. "You have caught a bird too."

As he spoke, he felt himself filling with jealousy. The blind man's bird was marvelously colored, as if it had flown through a rainbow and been stained by the colors. The feathers from a bird such as that would make a fine present for his new wife, but the blind man had a wife too, and she would also want the feathers.

The young man bent down and took the blind man's bird from the trap. Then, quickly substituting his own bird, he passed it to the blind man and put the colored bird into his own pouch.

"Here is your bird," he said to the blind man.

"You may put it in your pouch."

The blind man reached out for the bird and took it. He felt it for a moment, his fingers passing over the wings and the breast. Then, without saying anything, he put the bird into his pouch and they began the trip home.

On their way home, the two men stopped to rest under a broad tree. As they sat there, they talked about many things. The young man was impressed with the wisdom of the blind man, who knew a great deal although he could see nothing at all.

"Why do people fight with one another?" he asked the blind man. It was a question which had always troubled him, and he wondered if the blind man could give him an answer.

The blind man said nothing for a few moments, but it was clear to the young man that he was thinking. Then the blind man raised his head, and it seemed to the young man as if the unseeing eyes were staring right into his soul. Quietly he gave his answer.

"Men fight because they do to each other what you have just done to me."

The words shocked the young man and made him ashamed. He tried to think of a response, but none came. Rising to his feet, he fetched his pouch, took out the brightly colored bird, and gave it back to the blind man.

The blind man took the bird, felt over it with his fingers, and smiled.

"Do you have any other questions for me?" he asked.

"Yes," said the young man. "How do men become friends after they have fought?"

The blind man smiled again.

"They do what you have just done," he said. "That's how they become friends again."

* * *

Mr. Reaf ended up reading the story to each class. In every period the kids expressed some strong feelings about the characters. Most believed the blind man to be very wise. In sixth period Sanford got the biggest laugh of the day when he said the blind man ought to work as a security guard in a store. But Johnson took top honors for surprising Reaf the most. She took great offense that the birds were being captured and killed just for their feathers. Well, that got sixth period on the subject of using animals for nonessential purposes. Tanya yelled out that she had a right to wear a feather boa or a fur coat if she wanted to. Other kids started talking about everything from raising greyhounds for racing to killing animals for food. Who would have ever thought Rhonda Jackson would lecture the class on the amount of land it takes for Americans to raise cattle for beef? Where did she learn that? The last thing he remembered was Jose strutting out at the bell, yelling that he was going to turn in Juan's uncle for holding cockfights.

When the door slammed shut behind the last student, Reaf plopped down in his seat. He felt absolutely drained. Why had he agreed to talk to Luis after school? He just wanted to go home. Reaf decided to cut their talk short.

He sat behind his desk, drumming a pencil on top of his briefcase. Come on, he thought. Let's get this over with. It's Friday. Then the door groaned.

"Good afternoon, sir!" Luis said brightly. With broom in hand he shuffled directly over to the desk. Reaf reached for a stack of papers and straightened them as one would a deck of cards.

"Hello, Mr. Argueta. Look, I haven't got long. I have some things I need to do this afternoon. So we'll have to make this brief. Okay?"

"Certainly, sir. As long as you wish," he replied, smiling. "Did you try that story today?"

"Actually, I did."

"How did the students respond, if I may ask?"

"Well, they seemed to like it. What with the short periods and the assembly, we didn't have much time to discuss it. But thanks, anyway." Reaf paused. "Why did you want me to read an old folktale to these kids, anyway? You trying to teach them something?" he asked jokingly.

Luis smiled back. "Well, sir, you tell me. Did they learn anything?"

Reaf laughed and leaned back in his chair. "Oh, I don't know. They sure had a lot to say, but not about the story. Most of them wanted to talk about all sorts of stuff in their own lives. I wouldn't say they *learned* anything, really." He paused and looked at Luis seriously. "Why? What did you want them to get out of it?"

"Perhaps nothing more than they did, sir. But I do find much wisdom in that story. Did you not?"

Reaf opened his briefcase and tossed some papers inside. Without looking up, he said smugly, "It made an interesting point, I guess. But I think there might be more direct ways to teach wisdom in schools."

"Do you believe schools teach wisdom, sir?"

Reaf looked up at him. "Well, we try. At least to those kids who'll listen and behave. I gather you don't think we do?"

"I would say, sir, that most of what schools teach is knowledge, not wisdom."

"And the difference?" the teacher asked.

The janitor glanced around Reaf's desk. "Do you have a dictionary, sir?"

"Sure."

Opening the bottom drawer of his desk, Reaf pulled out a pocket-sized dictionary. He handed it to the janitor, who thumbed quickly through the pages, then paused and began to read silently. Holding that place with a finger, he thumbed to the back of the book and began to read again. Then he looked up at Reaf expectantly.

"If I may, sir?"

"Sure, go ahead."

Luis started reading aloud. "By definition, knowledge is

'the body of facts and principles accumulated by mankind.' " He flipped to the back of the book. "Wisdom is 'the power to choose the best course of action based on one's knowledge, experiences, values, and intuition.' " He shut the book. "In other words, Mr. Reaf, knowledge is only part of wisdom."

"Well, Argueta, in that case, what's wrong with our schools just teaching knowledge?"

Luis smiled. "Some would say, sir, that knowledge is based on the past. It deals only in experience. Wisdom, however, looks to the future. It dreams in possibilities. And in schools, Mr. Reaf, do we not want children to reach beyond their experiences, to dream?"

Reaf laughed. "As the kids say, Luis, 'Get real.' Most of these kids don't care about that stuff. They're just trying to get through each day. Shoot, most of them don't care about anything anymore."

Luis stared at Reaf for a moment in silence, then asked, "Mr. Reaf, would you mind if I sat down?"

"Sure, help yourself," the teacher said, motioning to the row of desks.

Leaning his broom against the wall, Luis picked up a large desk at the end of the row and brought it up beside Reaf's desk. Sliding into the seat he looked like a small child sitting in an oversized chair. His feet barely touched the ground. Luis looked up at Reaf with a serious expression on his face. "Mr. Reaf, may I ask you a question?"

"Yeah, sure."

"What do you care about?"

Reaf shifted uncomfortably in his seat. "What do you mean?"

"What do you value, Mr. Reaf? What are the most important things in your life?"

The teacher looked across the room, took a deep breath, and thought a moment. "Well, I guess first of all I value myself. I've learned to stand up for myself in this life, to stand by my beliefs, even if I've had to go it alone."

Luis nodded his head in agreement. "And what else do you value, sir?"

He picked up a pencil and began tapping it on his desk. "Well, I guess I value my family. I learned that when my brother was killed. Going through that really pulled us together. I don't know what I would have done without my mom and dad during those first months after David's death. I was so hurt, so confused. We really needed each other." He paused, thinking how often his parents had stood by him. "And then, when my wife left me, I realized again how important family can be. I don't just mean losing my wife, but, you know, the first person I called when she left was my mom." He looked down at his desk, at the old, tattered lesson-plan book.

"And I guess I value education, at least I used to. God knows I've given enough of my life to it. I know I act like an ogre around here, but deep down I want to believe that teaching kids is an admirable profession. It's just I don't know how to reach these kids anymore."

"So, Mr. Reaf, you are telling me you value family, learning, and yourself. Are these not wonderful things to teach our children? To learn to love and accept ourselves and our families. Is there not wisdom in this?"

He looked up at Luis. "Argueta, I'm telling you these kids don't care about that. Most of these kids could care less about what I try to teach in here. They don't want to learn. They don't even care about themselves or each other. God, just look at the drugs they're doing and how they're killing each other!"

"Are you saying, sir, that most of your students don't care about their families, or learning, or even themselves?"

"Well, they don't seem to," he said indignantly.

Luis reached into his back pocket and pulled out his wallet. His thin, delicate fingers began flipping through one of the folds, searching for something. He pulled out a small, folded piece of yellow paper. "Mr. Reaf, our behavior toward ourselves and others does not necessarily reflect who we really are. When I find myself judging others on their fearful actions, I reread this by Vincent Cronin."

He handed the teacher the piece of paper. Reaf read aloud the quote, written in that same meticulous script: "Our bodies contain three grams of iron, three grams of bright, silver-white manganese, and copper. Proportionate to size, they are among the weightiest atoms in our bodies, and they came from the same source, a long-ago star. There are pieces of stars within us all."

Reaf looked up into the janitor's face. Luis's eyes sparkled. "Mr. Reaf, did you not tell me your students were excited about the story they read today?"

"Yeah, well. So they get excited about one old folktale," he said, handing back the slip of paper. "Everyday can't be play day. They certainly don't get excited about *real* learning."

"And what is real learning, Mr. Reaf?"

He opened his mouth to say, "Grammar" but stopped. Luis smiled. He knew what the teacher was thinking. Embarrassed, Reaf rose and walked over to the bookshelf along the wall behind his desk. The shelves were crammed with old, dusty literature anthologies. He began to straighten the books.

"You'd like me to teach old folktales every day, wouldn't you?" he said accusingly, over his shoulder.

"Literature does offer some wonderful examples of both wise and unwise living, sir," Luis called out.

Reaf shook his head, pulled a book off the shelf, and turned to face Luis. "I'm not so sure about that, Argueta. Teachers have taught literature for years, and where has that gotten us? These stories don't change anyone."

"Perhaps, sir, that is not the fault of the stories. Perhaps it is how they are taught."

"You're wrong, Argueta. A number of my colleagues teach kids to analyze these stories."

Luis smiled. "Are you referring to the act of turning literature into test questions, sir?"

"No, no. They teach stuff, like irony, characterization, main idea, those sorts of things."

The janitor nodded. "Tell me, Mr. Reaf, what do you like to read?"

"Me? Well, I like mysteries. They're a good escape. And I guess my favorite novel is *The Grapes of Wrath*."

"Really, sir. Why do you like this book so much?"

"Oh, I just always admired the Joad family. They were so strong. They stuck by each other through all their hardships. Ma Joad was really something. You know the scene that really got to me was after they lost everything in Oklahoma and struck out for California to start a new life. Here they were, driving that old, rickety truck with all their belongings stacked on top of it across Death Valley at night so that the truck wouldn't overheat. And sometime in the middle of the night the grandma died in Ma Joad's arms. But Ma didn't say anything to the others. She just kept holding her. She knew how important it was that they keep going. Not until they got past the California border patrol did she let the others know Grandma was dead. Boy, that was powerful."

"It reminds you of your family, doesn't it, sir?"

"Yeah, I guess it does." Reaf paused, thinking about his own mom. Sometimes he missed her so much. She was one strong woman. He turned back toward the bookcase. This conversation was getting a little too personal for him. "So what do you like to read, Luis?"

"Well, sir, I must admit that *The Grapes of Wrath* is one of my favorite books, too."

He spun around, surprised at this last remark. "It is? I never figured--uh, I mean, why do you like it?"

Luis smiled. "Because, sir, I also see many similarities between the Joads and my life. I know what it is to wander, to want to work, to endure the hardships an outsider must endure in a new land."

"So, you like reading American literature?"

"I enjoy reading most great literature, Mr. Reaf. It is like eating at a buffet; I almost always find something that satisfies a hunger within me. I enjoy long works like *The Grapes of Wrath,* but I also enjoy reading old myths, legends, and folktales from around the world, like the one I gave you. I find these stories help me to learn to make wiser choices in my own life."

Reaf waved the book that he'd been holding at the janitor. "Argueta, what is your point here? Are you saying that we should just teach classic literature, like Steinbeck and folktales?"

Luis opened his hands toward the teacher. "Mr. Reaf, why should we limit ourselves? We can learn from many different kinds of literature."

"What modern writers would you suggest?" Reaf asked. "Give me an example."

Luis thought for a moment, then his eyes brightened. "Well, sir, just this morning I read a beautiful piece about the homeless in the newspaper. It was written by Anna Quindlen, a Pulitzer Prize-winning journalist. She described how basic it is to anyone's sanity to have a home--a place to call your own. Quite frankly, this piece meant a lot to me."

Reaf turned and shoved the literature book back on the shelf. "So what you're saying is that we should quit teaching math, science, and history, and teach nothing but literature? Let the kids ponder their navels and never learn any content."

Luis folded his hands in front of him and smiled. "Why would we stop teaching these other subjects, Mr. Reaf? We need people with these skills to save our world. But I think we should also give them the desire to save our world instead of just filling their own mouths and pockets. To do that we must consider how we teach something as well as what we teach."

Reaf walked back over to his desk and sat down hard in his seat. "And you really believe literature can do that, influence people, make them better?"

Luis smiled. "I believe good literature and good teaching can."

Reaf shook his head. "I used to, Argueta. I used to believe schools could make a difference. But now I think we mostly provide a holding pen for kids to grow up in. I mean, you more than anybody can see what a mess this school is. How can you honestly believe it can turn kids around, with all the other negative influences bearing down on them?"

Luis lowered his head a moment, then looked up and said softly, "Mr. Reaf, I can think of two answers to your question. First, we do not give enough credit to the power of caring teachers who create a loving space for children. The people in such schools, by their example, help children change their own lives. And that is how the world changes, one life at a time. Second, Mr. Reaf, we have no other choice. Schools must help turn things around, because we are losing too many of our children to drugs, to greed, to apathy, and to violence. And someday, Mr. Reaf, we will pay a very dear price for the way some of our children are growing up. As an old folktale tells us, 'When you starve with the tiger, the tiger eats last.' "

Reaf looked deep into Luis's eyes. "So, Mr. Argueta, you *are* here to try to change me, aren't you?"

Luis tossed his head back and laughed. "Mr. Reaf, one of the greatest tasks in life for any of us is to change ourselves. It would be extremely arrogant of me to think I could change another human being. Influence you, perhaps. Change, no; that is something only you can do. But, sir, sharing my ideas with you forces me to look deeply into my own beliefs and values. Your questions help me better understand and possibly change my own life."

"Well, Mr. Argueta, maybe I've been under the wrong impression for fifteen years, but what's the job of the teacher if not to change children?"

"Maybe, sir, it is simply to create a loving space where children can consider the ideas, values, and beliefs of others with compassion and respect. Perhaps the Dalai Lama of Tibet said it best, Mr. Reaf: 'If you can, help others; if you cannot do that, at least do not harm them.' "

Reaf leaned forward on the desk and cupped his head in his hands. So much, so much. This man says so much. It all sounds so right, but what am I supposed to do? He glanced down at his watch. Good God, where had the time gone?

"I hope I haven't kept you too long?" Luis asked.

"No, no. But I guess I should be going." Feeling a bit shell-shocked, he grabbed his briefcase and headed around the desk. As he pulled on the metal door, he yelled above the groaning hinges, "Mr. Argueta, tell me in one sentence why I should listen to you."

For the first time that afternoon Luis took his gaze completely away from the teacher. Looking out the small window across the room, he said, "Mr. Reaf, if in some school a certain gang of teenagers had been taught some wisdom and compassion, your brother might still be alive today."

Reaf froze in the doorway. A painful lump filled his throat. Luis turned to look at him. The teacher looked down at his feet.

"What you ask seems so huge," he mumbled. "How would I ever begin to change?"

"Mr. Reaf?"

He looked up at Luis, who was smiling.

"Perhaps you might follow Socrates' advice: When a young man asked him on the road, 'How can I reach Mount Olympus?' Socrates replied simply, 'Just make sure every step you take goes in that direction.' "

Reaf laughed, shaking his head. "Argueta, how in the hell do you remember all these sayings?"

Like a flower closing at twilight, the smile slowly disappeared from his face. "Mr. Reaf, I remember them because I try to live them."

"Yeah, why not," the teacher said and let the door close quietly behind him.

Mr. Reaf spent the weekend home alone.

Week Three, Day One

Wet. Cold wetness. Why am I wet?

Reaf rolled over on his back, his cheek still tingling with the damp chill, his mind searching for meaning like a hand reaching in a mailbox for a hoped-for letter. Slowly, another feeling rose into his consciousness--a heavy feeling, pressing, pulling him down, leaden, sinking, quicksand.

He knew this feeling, this deep sadness. He also knew how to avoid it. He would drink or work, go to a movie or sleep. But sleep didn't always work. You could lose control while asleep. You couldn't protect yourself while asleep. He rolled back over on his side.

Wet. Cold wetness. He opened his eyes and raised himself up on his elbow. The pillow was damp. Why?

Then the dream began to come back in strobe like images: the moonlight rippling on the black water of a mountain lake. The campfire licking the night sky with yellow tongues. The orange tent glowing like a furnace under the trees. And David, sitting beside him, laughing and patting him on the back.

He wants to stop him, to tell him something, but David just keeps laughing. Reaf can't get the words out. Then, from the cocoon of sleeping bags, David tells him in his rich, deep voice, "Good night." He listens to the click and rattle of the creatures of the night replace the sputtering of the last log on the fire. Sleep.

Suddenly his eyes are open wide. David! He's gone! He's out there somewhere. Got to find him. Panic, scrambling to get out of the sleeping bag, but it's become a straightjacket that wraps his arms and legs around him. He feels as if he's suffocating. He fights to get his head outside the tent and gasp for cool air.

"David!" he calls out into the night. But all is black and endless.

“David, come back!” But all is still and silent.

“David,” he whispers and crawls back down into his sleeping bag, shaking with fear, praying he’ll answer, he’ll return. Then the cold wetness on his pillow, a salty taste in his mouth, and a heavy sadness in his heart.

Mr. Reaf got up and dressed for school.

* * *

The morning hallway felt like being in a panic-stricken school of fish. Students pushed, pulled, laughed, and screamed. Reaf bounced in semiconsciousness like a pinball through the crowd, slowly making his way to first period. After his weekend home alone, he felt dizzy, lost, overwhelmed by the humanity that surrounded him. Suddenly, someone seized his arm.

“Mr. Reaf? Excuse me, Mr. Reaf? I hate to bother you, but I didn’t see you last Friday and I have two quick things I need to say to you.”

He turned to face Mrs. Hurren. She stood there staring at him intently as he rolled with the punches from the teeming hallway.

“First, please ask your sixth-period class to pick up after themselves at the end of each day.”

He looked at her, confused. “Why?”

“Well, it’s these budget cuts. The principal called that nice little janitor in last week and let him go.”

“What?” he yelled. A number of heads turned his way. Mrs. Hurren instinctively took a step back.

“Well, Mr. Reaf, I realize it is an inconvenience, but your students will--”

“Mrs. Hurren, what do you mean he was let go?”

“Well, Mr. Argueta was fired. I’m upset about it, too, especially after what some students told me about him.”

Her words seemed more and more distant. How could Luis be gone? What would he do? His eyes focused on a bulletin board down the hall announcing the upcoming achievement tests.

"It seems that Mr. Argueta is a homeless person."

Reaf's eyes whipped back to her. "What! What are you talking about?" he said angrily. "Mrs. Hurren, are you playing some kind of joke on me?"

"No, I'm afraid not, Mr. Reaf. Some students saw Mr. Argueta washing his clothes at a local laundromat and then climbing into his car. They sneaked by to check on him, and he was asleep in the back seat."

"But, Mrs. Hurren, how did he even get a job here without giving a street address?" he asked skeptically.

"Well, I wondered the same thing, so I asked the school secretary. She said that on his application Mr. Argueta wrote 'A' Street in the space for local address."

Thoughts, images, and feelings about the little man came at Reaf faster than he could handle them. He reached out for the wall to steady himself. Mrs. Hurren stepped closer and took his arm.

"Mr. Reaf, are you all right?"

He looked at her. "No, I'm not, Mrs. Hurren."

"Is there anything I can do?" she said sincerely.

"I think I should just go to class."

"Oh, certainly. But just one more thing, Mr. Reaf. I hate to bother you with this now, but I simply must have your textbook order. Now, you have a choice between--"

"Order the literature books, Mrs. Hurren."

"Are you sure?" she asked uncertainly.

"Order the literature books, Mrs. Hurren."

The late bell rang. He turned away from Mrs. Hurren, who stood there with her mouth wide open. A cold drizzle had begun to fall as he hurried across the courtyard to his quonset hut and first period. He shuddered from both the cold and his own uncertainty.

Almost at a run, Reaf lowered his shoulder to push the heavy metal door open. Unexpectedly, the door gave way easily, and he was catapulted into the room. He sailed right for Joanna, who sat just inside. As she covered her head, he somehow caught his balance and stopped, teetering over her. The class broke into laughter. Stung, he glared at them. They quieted down immediately. He was in no mood to play.

Suddenly, he heard the door fly open behind him. He was knocked to the side as a tall figure flew into the room, ricocheted off Reaf, and landed half on the floor and half in Joanna's lap. The teacher looked down to see Tom, who obviously had been late to class, leaning over Joanna and gasping for air. His hot breath was not more than an inch from her breasts. A sly smile crept across his face. He rolled his eyes upward to meet hers. Without flinching, Joanna said loudly, "When pigs fly, Tom, when pigs fly."

Reaf burst into laughter. The class followed suit. Tom slid to the floor, shook his head, then pulled himself up and walked with head bowed toward his seat. As Reaf headed for his desk he called out, "Who fixed the door?"

"We don't know," returned Paul. "We figured you finally had it fixed."

"It sure makes it easier to come into your classroom," called out Rachel.

He turned to Rachel. "I have a distinct feeling that was the person's intention."

Turning to his desk, he stopped dead in his tracks. The desk was spotless. Gone were the scattered pencils and paper clips, the old styrofoam coffee cups, the leftover sandwich wrappings, the rubber bands. But the most noticeable thing missing was the chalk dust, the accumulated pedagogical pollen from years of teaching swept clean away. The desk had not only been wiped clean but polished. It literally glistened. In the center was one book. And on top of it was an envelope. He moved the envelope to see the book's title--*Bartlett's Familiar Quotations*.

"Mr. Reaf?"

He looked up. "Yes, Paul?"

"Do you really want us to discuss today's quote?"

Reaf looked quickly at the board. There, written in that same meticulous script was Luis's final quote.

> The future will depend on what we do in the present.
>
> --Mahatma Gandhi

He smiled. The class sat watching him, waiting for an answer to Paul's question. He turned to Paul. "Absolutely. Why wouldn't we?"

"But, Mr. Reaf," called out Paul, "I mean, it's such an obvious point. Why discuss it?"

He thought about what Luis had said. Make them relate the ideas to their own lives.

"Paul, it may seem obvious, but I have a feeling that there isn't a soul in this room who hasn't messed up a piece of his or her future by not taking advantage of the present. Who hasn't had regrets about not having done something when he had the chance?"

"How 'bout you, Mr. Reaf?" called out Tom with that wise-guy tone of his. He had finally found his seat. "So 'fess up. What is one of your regrets?"

Instantly he thought of his brother. The class stared at him, wondering if he would reply. He tried quickly to think of another example, but his mind went blank. He looked back up at the board. "The future will depend on what we do in the present." He cleared his throat.

"Tom, I regret not having told my brother that I loved him before he was murdered. If I had done that, I might not have felt so guilty and sad all these years."

Tom's mouth fell open. The eyes in the room became full moons. You could have heard the proverbial pin plummet to the floor. Reaf tried to cough away the lump in his throat.

"Okay, your turn. In your notebook, describe an instance when you didn't do something in the present moment that later affected your future."

"Does it have to be something sad?" asked Rachel.

"Absolutely not, Rachel. If you've made a good decision about something, please share it with us. Maybe we'll all learn something."

They sat motionless.

"Any problems with that?"

A number of kids mumbled, "No, sir."

"Then get to work."

He watched as papers and pens appeared and students began to scribble uncertainly. Then he sat down and picked up the envelope. His hands were shaking as he slipped his finger behind the flap to tear it open. Inside was a small slip of paper, a note, written in that same beautiful script.

> Mr. Reaf,
>
> I hope you don't mind my straightening up a bit. I thought you might want to begin the week with a clean start. Changing our physical surroundings has a wonderful way of helping us see new possibilities.
>
> As I guess you've heard, I will also be experiencing some changes in my life, seeing new possibilities. I must admit that I am sad we did not have more time to talk. You helped me listen to my own heart.
>
> If, in the future, you should feel unsure of your focus when so many others approach you with their own needs and agendas, then hold this last quote in your heart and listen to the wisdom it teaches.
>
> "Everything you teach you are learning. Teach only love, and learn that love is yours and you are love."
>
> --*A Course in Miracles*
>
> P.S. I fixed your door.
> Most respectfully,
> Luis Argueta

A small plop sounded as a single tear landed on the page. Mr. Reaf pressed the letter against his chest, then folded it neatly and slipped it into his wallet.

"Okay, how are we doing with our quote? Who has something to share?"

Hands shot up around the room.

About the Author

Bill McBride drew on many of his own professional experiences to write *Entertaining an Elephant*. He has worked in a variety of public school and university settings. In middle and secondary schools he has served as a reading specialist, English and Drama teacher, Gifted and Talented instructor, and curriculum coordinator. Bill won numerous awards for his teaching skills. On the university level, Bill assisted in the training and evaluation of middle and secondary English teachers. He holds a Ph.D. from the University of North Carolina at Chapel Hill.

Though he grew up in the South, Bill has lived in places as varied as Germany and Illinois. He spent six years in Chicago working as an editor and writer of language arts textbooks. Currently he makes his living as a national language arts consultant for McDougal Littell, the secondary textbook division of Houghton Mifflin publishing company. Bill is known nationwide as a speaker and presenter of innovative teaching methodologies. He lives in San Francisco with his cat.